AGAINST THE WIND

McAnally Flats Press
4809 Riversedge Road
Louisville, TN 37777
www.McAnallyFlatsPress.com

Library of Congress Control Number: 2016910977
ISBN: 978-0-9819209-4-8
Copyright information available upon request
v. 1.0

Cover Design: MSDesigns / Shutterstock and Everett Historical
Interior Design: J. L. Saloff
Typography: Minion Pro, Bordeaux Roman Bold

First Edition, 2016
Printed on acid free paper in the United States of America.

Peter, Tyler, and Trey

Also by Larry Henry:

Garden of Eden

Plato's Cave

Noah's Ark

AGAINST THE WIND

Larry Henry

MCANALLY FLATS PRESS

1940

"What General Weygand called the Battle of France is over... the Battle of Britain is about to begin. Upon this battle depends the survival of Christian civilization. Upon it depends our own British life and the long continuity of our institutions and our Empire. The whole fury and might of the enemy must very soon be turned on us. Hitler knows that he will have to break us in this island or lose the war. If we can stand up to him, all Europe may be freed and the life of the world may move forward into broad, sunlit uplands. But if we fail, then the whole world, including the United States, including all that we have known and cared for, will sink into the abyss of a new dark age made more sinister, and perhaps more protracted, by the lights of perverted science. Let us therefore brace ourselves to our duties, and so bear ourselves, that if the British Empire and its Commonwealth last for a thousand years, men will still say, This Was Their Finest Hour."

Winston Churchill

Chapter One

The Bayou

Moses Blue Pony sat quietly on his back porch watching the sun set among the cypress trees. The swamp was motionless, with the occasional cry of a heron and the chorus of the frogs. Colors sliced through the trees, gold and orange, reds and yellows, as the sun sank lower and lower between the branches. Dusk fell and the fireflies came out, blinking their yellow messages. Moses was at peace with his world, enjoying the pictorial splendor of his Louisiana autumn.

The year was 1990. Moses Blue Pony had been home from the Vietnam War for 18 years. Moses had killed nine men in the jungles of Indochina during his two tours of duty. The one he remembered most was a Vietcong butcher he scalped and left tied to a tree for the tigers to eat. The VC had hacked off the arms of seven little children because an American medic had given them vaccination shots.

Max, his blind cocker spaniel, lay at his feet fast asleep. The dog would whimper now and then, moving her hind legs, chasing squirrels when she was a younger dog. The pit bull, her constant company, lay still beside the raggedy old porch couch, keeping watch over his master and his blind friend. The pit bull weighed half as much as Blue Pony, but he was lean and agile for a dog his size and age. Moses called him White Devil. The dog had been trained by a breeder to protect cattle and horses against predators. The breeder got himself killed in a roadside tavern, and the dog was badly injured. The animal was about to be put down, but Moses prevailed and brought the dog home. The three of them were companions now.

Swamp Kat, an old swamp kitty, lay curled up beside Moses on the couch. The Indian absentmindedly stroked the cat's ratty-looking fur. The cat had scars all over her body. She'd survived numerous battles with foxes and coons intent on eating her. Swamp Kat weighed fifteen pounds. She followed Moses and the dogs wherever they went.

Blue Pony observed headlights approaching down the abandoned logging trail. That would be his friend from town bringing beans and salt pork and more beer. Blue Pony owned no automobile. But he did have electricity, and a new window unit to cool his log cabin during the humid months of summer. The man from town was a retired Navy flyer who had been wounded during the war. He and Blue Pony shared a mutual dislike for lawyers and politicians. His name was Karl Musgrove. He walked with a limp from a piece of shrapnel embedded against his lower spine. But he was a cheerful fellow. He and the Cherokee had become friends in Vietnam. Musgrove became a real estate agent after the war. Blue Pony had purchased the ninety-acre spread from Karl. The cabin and land had been on the market for several years. Nobody wanted to live in the swamp. Moses Blue Pony loved his ninety-acre paradise.

"White Devil! Come here, big man!"

The pit bull jumped up, placing his front paws on Karl's midsection, nearly knocking the man down.

"I got you a treat, old fellow."

Karl walked back to his truck, bringing out a bone from the butcher shop in town. Then he carried the groceries and beer up on the porch.

"You want these inside?"

"Yes, please. Put on table."

Karl came back outside, pulling out his pipe. He stuffed it with Turkish tobacco and lit up.

"There's a square dance in town Saturday night. You oughta come."

"Me no good with strangers. I stay home."

"You'll never get a woman out here in the sticks. We got pretty ladies in town. They'd like a big Injun hero."

"Me no hero. Just old Army grunt."

"That Silver Star inside says different. I'll come fetch ya."

One thousand and seventy-six miles northeast, James Cohen sat at his antique mahogany desk, gloating over his latest political achievement. A $648 million Green Energy project between Nevada, California, and the Communist Chinese had just been ratified by Congress. Cohen's K Street connections, plus a few greased palms, had paid off handsomely. Republicans and Democrats were both onboard. A leather briefcase atop his desk contained $775,000, his reward from various senators and foreign contractors for putting the deal together. The general public would bear the expense: those he looked down upon as little people, the dupes, the suckers, men and women too stupid to comprehend reality. He loved Washington, DC. A person could make a fortune there, being in the right place at the right time.

Taking the elevator down, he spoke briefly with Security at the front desk. Outside, he took the shortcut to his Mercedes, through the alleyway. The stars were pale points of light in an early night sky. The moon was coming up, a beautiful setting for the Magician of K Street, whom so many others wished to emulate. He was indeed one of a kind. His financial and political intrigues were legend. An attractive platinum blonde waited for him at their Foggy Bottom rendezvous. He carried a piece of emerald jewelry in his vest pocket for Joyce.

Sauntering through the alleyway, he envisioned Joyce naked, kneeling before him on the marble balcony of his condominium overlooking the Potomac River. Her firm, ripe breasts intrigued him. She was young and filled with an insatiable sexual appetite. He would use her up then find himself a new playmate, a redhead perhaps, or maybe a big-breasted Southern brunette. Women were all alike to him, there for his personal gratification until he tired of their emotional nonsense. He had no time for emotions, just money, power, his Marxist friends, and personal glory in the land of the politicians.

A shadow stepped out from behind the Dumpster as he passed by. Another appeared from a doorway. He didn't hear or see them until it was too late. The tall one placed a gloved hand over his mouth and another hand around his throat while the shorter man shoved an ice pick into the base of his skull, once, twice, three times. The Magician of K Street kicked briefly, peed his pants, quivered, and died. They dragged him over to a Honda rental, and shoved him into the trunk. His leather briefcase was placed on the backseat. Then they departed as casually as they had arrived.

⌒

Down in Buckhead, Georgia, Zelda Henry, age ten going on eighteen, was exclaiming to her grandfather her excitement over a musical group she had just discovered the week before, Roxette, the Swedish rock duo.

"Oh golly, she's so good. I just love her. And her guitar player, he's sooo handsome. She sings a song called "Dangerous." It's so cool. Do you think I'm dangerous, Gran-paw?"

"About as dangerous as a cocked pistol. Men are gonna fall all over themselves when you come out."

"Will we have my debutante party at the country club, Gran-paw?"

"Yes, we'll have it at the country club. I'll invite my friends from Miami, and all over."

"Will Mister Cottonmouth come too, please?"

"Yes, Mister Cottonmouth will come. Harry, Bootnose, and Rico, all those fellows who protected your mama and daddy before you were born. They were here when you were four, remember?"

"I remember when the bad man came in the window and the big man grabbed him."

"That was John Franklin, the one they call Cottonmouth, protecting you and Zephyr."

"Do you think they'll try to hurt us again, Gran-paw?"

"No, Mister Rico took care of that. They won't be back. It's bedtime, young lady. Get on upstairs now."

"Yes, Gran-paw." Zelda kissed his cheek and scampered out of the library.

Winston Peters leaned back in his easy chair, remembering the life he'd led: B-17 bomber pilot, flying black market supplies around Africa and the South Pacific, then back to Atlanta with Trudy and Dutch, protecting them from the killers. That last encounter had been a close one until Rico flew in with his crew. They killed every last one of them. That sent a message. Zelda and Zephyr and his family were off limits.

Winston Peters was 68 years old, no longer a spry young pilot. He needed protection from those who might seek revenge on him and his family. Enrico Basilio, his Mafia pal in Miami, was a good man to have in one's corner. Rico was twenty years younger. John Franklin was forty-nine, but still a fearsome individual. Winston might need them again someday, judging from the evolving patterns in Washington, DC, and around the world.

⌒

Fat Mike in Miami took the call from Ruth Townsend at CIA headquarters in Langley, Virginia. Both telephone lines were secure. The two communicated only when something was needed or a problem had arisen. Adolfo D'Angelo and Frado were driving to Slidell with the body of James Cohen.

"A package is en route for our friend. Can you make that connection?"

"Yes. Thank you."

Both lines went dead. They seldom talked more than a few seconds, in case some whiz kid had figured out a way to tap either phone. Fat Mike called Rico to inform him of their success. Rico gave Mike the number to contact Adolfo on his car phone. That line was secure too.

Karl Musgrove answered Adolfo's telephone call on the second ring. "Hello."

"We have a package to deliver."

"Okay, meet me at the silo on the side of the highway. Same place as last time. I'll lead you in."

"We'll be there in about an hour. We're fifty-five miles out.

"Roger, over and out."

Karl slipped on the shoulder holster he wore as an F-14 fighter pilot. No use taking chances if the wrong people showed up, like a crooked cop or some bonehead coonass looking for an easy score. The .45 had pearl handles and held eight rounds. A second clip he attached to his leather holster held seven rounds.

Karl would lead them south on Interstate 59 until they reached the turnoff into the bayou country. At the end of a paved county road it was an eight-mile stretch into the swamp. It was never safe to walk in there after dark, too many snakes and alligators lurking about.

Chapter Two

Mister K Street

A slight drizzle was coming down as Karl Musgrove, Frado, and Adolfo D'Angelo drove along the logging trail toward Moses Blue Pony's cabin. The cabin had once served as the field office for a logging operation. That was years ago. The road was rough now, grown over with weeds and prickly briars. Karl pulled his pickup truck into the first turnaround which was a large open field. A deer flushed and ran away in the dark.

"Put your package in the truck bed. It's too rough for a car."

Adolfo popped the trunk lid then he and Frado loaded the body into the pickup. James Cohen was wrapped in plastic to keep from soiling the trunk of the rental car. Cohen was stiff. Rigor was setting in.

Adolfo spoke. "We got orders to head on back. You take care of Mister K Street."

Frado stepped forward and handed Karl a plastic sack. "Rico said give you this."

"Drive careful, men. The cops down here are real assholes."

Blue Pony was waiting on the porch. Karl had telephoned ahead with his cell phone.

"Let's go inside and see what we got," Karl said.

Karl dumped the sack on the table. Out tumbled twenty bundles of hundred dollar bills, fifty bills to a bundle. Karl counted one of the bundles.

"My God, Moses. That's $100,000."

"I get Mason jars. We bury under rose bushes."

"You gonna wax the lids?"

"Sure, I'll melt candles. Let's see what's in truck."

They stripped the body, all but his briefs, taking his watch and rings, the emerald brooch, a wallet, shoes, clothing, and Cohen's belt. The drizzle had stopped. Moses poured coal oil over the plastic, piling on twigs and dry wood and set it ablaze. They fed everything into the flames except the body, the jewelry, the brooch, and the belt buckle. Karl stirred the fire until only ashes remained.

A golden sun was making its dawn appearance when they loaded Mister Cohen into the bottom of the bass boat alongside Blue Pony's fishing pier. Moses cranked up his 25-horse Johnson, and they motored out into the bayou. Cypress trees rose majestically in every direction with garlands of Spanish moss hanging from their branches. The drifting fog above the silent, brackish waters gave the swamp an air of ghostly intrigue. It reminded Karl of a place to be avoided.

"Over there. See 'im?"

"That is the biggest goddamn thing I ever saw."

Moses stopped the motor and let the boat drift toward the animal.

When they were within a hundred feet, they eased the body over the gunwale into the water. Then Moses paddled back a few feet. The alligator smelled blood and slid down his muddy embankment into the swamp.

The monster came up beneath the body, grabbed hold, and shook the corpse violently. Cohen's head flew off, landing at Karl's feet in the bottom of the boat.

"Shit! Get me outta here!" Karl flung the head overboard.

Moses Blue Pony was bent over double, laughing. He engaged the motor and drove away.

Karl trailed his hands in the water, washing off the blood. "Well, I don't think it's funny."

"We get you job on television, make big money."

Karl raised his chin in defiance. "I am surrounded by people of questionable character!"

"I'll be manager, get you a stiff ever' week."

Karl finally smiled. "I guess it was kinda funny at that."

They tossed the metal objects into one of the deeper channels, and headed for the cabin.

Chapter Three

Birthday Girl

The United States was birthed in gunpowder and the blood of patriots. From the ashes of 1776 rose a nation of men and women who cherished God and country. Eighty-five years later, a civil war was fought between the Yankees and the Confederates over taxation without representation and slavery. The North defeated the South, the slaves were freed, and the carpetbaggers headed for Dixie.

The year 1917 saw Black Jack Pershing leading American doughboys on the battlefields of France against the armies of Kaiser Wilhelm. Germany was beaten after four years of bloodshed, then saddled with a flawed peace treaty which brought financial chaos and ruin to its German citizens. Because of that self-serving blunder by the Allies, Adolf Hitler became the Fuhrer of Nazi Germany.

Siberian armies and a freezing winter broke the back of Hitler's Barbarossa at Stalingrad in 1942. The battle of Kursk in 1943 sealed Hitler's fate. World War II would continue for two more years, consuming the lives of sixty to eighty million. Winston Churchill saved England, and probably the entire world.

Joseph Stalin died in 1953, presumably poisoned by Beria, chief of the secret police. It was feared Stalin was going to start a war with the Americans over the Berlin Airlift and Korea. Nikita Khrushchev became premier of the Soviet Union in 1958. In 1961 he gave his blessing for the construction of the Berlin Wall.

Russian propaganda emphasized it was to keep out anti-Soviet dissidents. In reality, it was to stop a brain drain of East Germans fleeing communism. The two Vietnam wars consumed another three and a half to five million people. In 1989 the Berlin blockade was finally recognized as a political liability, and East Berliners were allowed to visit the West. The wall came down in 1990. East and West Germany were reunited for the first time since 1945.

Ronald Reagan and Margaret Thatcher had triumphed. The Cold War was nearing an end.

Saddam Hussein invaded Kuwait in 1990. The stage was set once again for Uncle Sam to step into the breach. President Bush and his cabinet feared that Iraq was going to invade Saudi Arabia in an attempt to control the Arab oil fields and the Persian Gulf.

⸺

Commander Donavan had secured his platoon of four M1A1 Abrams battle tanks in the shadow of a high sand dune. They shut down their engines, opened their hatches, and sat listening for the approach of the Russian T-72 and the Chinese 69 tanks. A Pisces moon beamed down on the desert landscape, turning the dunes into a sea of shadowy mystery. Beneath the sand lay the bones of armies past.

"Out yonder ways, skipper, 'bout two miles, I'd say."

Billy Ray Donavan spoke quietly into his mic. "Crank 'em up, boys."

The steel monsters rumbled to life, forming a skirmish line eighty yards across. Thermal imaging revealed fifteen enemy tanks approaching at 2,400 meters. Most were Russian, a few Chinese, and one half-track carrying crates of ammunition.

"On my count … Three … two … one … Fire!"

It took one point five two seconds for four depleted uranium spikes to strike their intended targets. Molten steel and splinters ricocheted wildly inside the enemy turrets. One exploded, blasting his turret high into the night sky. Electronic range finders locked on to four more of the Republican Guards. The Abrams' gunners engaged. A single 125mm round struck Donavan's sloped front armor, glancing away and exploding. A second shell hit Cotton's tank. It, too, was ineffective. In seventy seconds, twelve Iraqi tanks were blasted into fiery twisted scrap metal, on fire and burning. The other three turned and fled.

"Get that half-track, John Boy."

The ammo crates exploded, sending a mushroom spiraling skyward.

They were twenty kilometers west of Kuwait, just inside the Iraq border, north of Saudi Arabia. Their assignment was to recon and report enemy positions. Invasion was to commence at 0400 hours. Commander Donavan radioed headquarters, explaining the vulnerability of the enemy armor. The Russian and Chinese tanks were no match for the heavily armored Abrams.

The Allied air campaign was having devastating effects as well, evidenced by a bombed-out 155mm Russian artillery battery. Dead men lay scattered around the gun emplacement, their bodies bloated and black from the desert sun.

"Let's head west and see what turns up."

Minutes later they came upon a wide berm cut deep into the desert floor. A tank trap. Huge oil drums were camouflaged with mesh netting and covered over with sand, making them invisible from the air. Oil would be flooded into the ditch then set ablaze once the Americans and their Allies became bogged down in the trenches.

Commander Donavan radioed HQ a second time. "It's plenty big enough to stop a tank. Yes, sir, bulldozers would work well. I'll light a few up for ya."

"Pick an oil drum, fellas. Use your fifties."

Each of the four Abrams gunners fired their .50 caliber machine guns into the giant drums. Tracer rounds ignited the volatile oil, sending boiling orange flames high into a star-spangled void.

"Skipper, we better get the hell outta here. Them ragheads ain't gonna be too happy with us punchin' holes in their damn barrels."

They turned south and drove for the border. The ground war would commence in two hours.

⤿

Trudy Peters sat before her vanity mirror, fussing with her makeup and brushing her blonde hair for the party. Not too shabby, she reasoned, for a thirty-nine-year-old gal with twin ten-year-olds and a devoted and adorable husband. She had worked hard to regain her girlish figure after giving birth to Zephyr and Zelda. Making love with Dutch was just as wonderful today as when they first made love onboard that boat. Trudy loved the way he always held her afterward.

She thought back to another crazy event, when she and Sarah helped Dutch and Boogie defend their cargo ship against those awful pirates. Firing that big gun was exciting, but she nearly got herself killed in the process. So did Sarah. They were lucky they weren't all killed. What an adventure that had been!

It happened again six years ago. An enemy of her father, with the Soviet Council of Ministers, who resented Winston's having helped certain countries with his black-market activities, had attempted to have him and his family assassinated. Winston's CIA friends got wind of events and warned Winston just in time. Rico was called and flew into Atlanta that same night. The men he brought with him were characters straight out of a James Bond thriller.

Harry Vento, the blue-eyed Mafia killer. She recalled Harry had been extremely cordial to her and the children. Bootnose, who walked with a limp and carried a sawed-off shotgun. He, too, was a gentleman in her presence. Adolfo D'Angelo, the tall one with black hair and black eyes and always a happy smile on his face. Strangely, she liked them all. But her favorite was the big man they called Cottonmouth. He was frightening to look at, but she knew right away that he was there for her and the girls.

He'd looked down at her, took her hand, and said the oddest thing. "I'll stay with the kiddies. You stay in the library with Poppa."

She did as she was told. Dutch was out of town so he didn't know.

At three o'clock in the morning she jerked awake when she heard glass breaking. Winston grabbed her arm, warning her to remain silent. Gunfire and yelling! Afterward there were four dead KGB men in the yard. None of Rico's friends got hurt. Rico came into the library, telling them it was okay to come out. The police arrived. Because of Winston's connections, they helped Rico's men load the bodies into a police van.

Rico had the dead men shipped back to Moscow, to the man who sent them. When the Soviet Council found out what Ivan Lipovsky had done, he disappeared.

The party tonight would include those same individuals, plus several others, some of whom she'd never met. Winston had gone all out, chilled Maine lobster tails and Gulf shrimp, Russian caviar, hearts of palm, seasoned roast beef, champagne, deviled eggs, French wine, imported brandy and vodka, North Sea salmon, the works. Her personal favorite was banana pudding, but she wouldn't disappoint Winston by telling him.

Dutch walked into the bedroom and stood behind his wife. "Wanna fool around, hot pants?"

Trudy laughed, stood up, and kissed her husband sweetly. "You always know the right thing to say."

"I had myself good teacher. You, in Panama."

"I'm looking forward to Sarah and Boogie. I wish John Paul and Pilar could come."

"Me too, but he has his army career to attend to."

"Is Rico still coming?"

"Yes, he's bringing part of the crew."

"You know, Dutch, for being a Mafia guy, Rico sure doesn't fit the mold. He's really nice."

"They're not all bad. Look at John Franklin. He's killed a lot of men, and he's as decent as they come."

"I just love him. He saved our babies that night."

"I'm sure glad he was here. I wish I'd been."

"You didn't know. None of us did until the last minute."

"Well, let's get downstairs. It's about time for our guests."

Harry Vento's wife, Doctor Margot Bach, had just turned forty-three. Winston's party was in her honor. CIA directors Ruth Townsend and George Brown were present, as was General Jack Marshal with the Joint Chiefs of Staff in Washington. Ruth and George had helped create the secret association ten years earlier in Winston's library. Rico had sponsored Doctor Bach in 1983.

The group's purpose was to protect the United States against communism, Islam, and American quislings. When exposure of a serious threat proved fruitless, a vote was taken. If the group deemed a man or woman to be a direct threat to the United States, Rico would send out two of his crew to do away with that person. Bodies were never left behind nor had one ever been recovered. Numerous individuals were involved with the project, including Lydia Sams with MI-6 in London, England, and Uriah Frank with the Israeli Mossad in Tel Aviv, Israel.

Ruth Townsend was quietly discussing a matter with Winston,

Rico, and Cottonmouth in front of a salt-water aquarium beside the fireplace in the living room. Ruth and George had uncovered another plot.

"The woman is a mole inside our State Department, stealing top-secret information for the Chinese government in Beijing. Her superior was discreetly informed twice. He keeps requesting official documentation. We can't divulge that information or we'd expose ourselves and our sources. That union moron doesn't know who we are anyway, so our end is secure."

"What was tha vote?" Cottonmouth asked.

Ruth replied, "The vote was unanimous."

Rico went to fetch Harry, bringing him over to join the group.

"We want you to put another team together."

"Same as last time, boss?"

"Yes, Harry." Ruth placed a hand on Harry's shoulder. "I'll get those addresses for you, and her work schedule."

~

Zephyr was in the library with Zelda and Winston. Dutch was at work. Trudy had gone to the supermarket up in Sandy Springs. The girls were discussing school, and how much they liked or disliked mathematics. They were also talking about their eleventh birthday.

"I hate math and logarithms and square roots. I hate all of it!"

Zephyr taunted Zelda. "You were born last so I got all the brains. Math is cool."

"Yes, but I'm the prettiest."

Zephyr became agitated. "That's not fair. I got daddy's nose, and you got mama's."

"Big Nose! Big Nose!"

"Girls, stop this bickering. You're both beautiful, noses and all."

"Well, she started it."

"Zelda, hush up now. Apologize to your sister."

"It's not fair. She called me stupid."

"Neither one of you is stupid. You're both bright young ladies."

"Okay. I'm sorry."

"Zephyr?"

"Oh all right, me too."

"Now, about those birthdays."

"Can we have it here, Gran-paw? Can we? Can we, please?"

"We can have it anywhere you want. Six Flags, right here, Joe Tierney's restaurant."

Zephyr made her request. "I like here best, Gran-paw.

Zelda agreed with her twin sister. "I do too, Gran-paw."

"Then here it shall be."

⁓

Desert Storm commenced February 24, 1991, at the prescribed hour of 0400. US Marines led the assault, assisted by thousands of tanks, armored personnel carriers, mobile artillery, fighting vehicles, and several armored bulldozers for breaching Saddam Hussein's tank traps and fortified bunkers. Forty-one nations joined the Coalition, led by the United States with over 500,000 US troops.

Captain Donavan's four Abrams and Major Hollingberry's three Challenger tanks were headed north along the western border of Kuwait in search of mobile Scud launchers. The Soviet Scud was not an accurate weapon, but they caused widespread panic inside Israel, Saudi Arabia, and Bahrain. Mounted on mobile carriers, it was easy to hide them under bridges or inside storage facilities.

"Commander Hollingberry. Over there, on your left. Check it out."

"By Godfrey, sir. That was a bit of bother."

"Raghead stew."

"Poor blokes. One of our aircraft cooked their chicken."

"That's 'cooked their goose,' but close enough."

They journeyed on in the general direction of the southern Iraqi city of Suq al-Shuyukh. The night air was crisp and cool. The desert sands resembled a vast ocean beneath the shining stars.

"Up ahead, skipper. Looks like trouble."

"Hollingberry, you see that?"

"Righto, Commander! Disperse to your right, mates."

Billy Ray Donavan swung his platoon left. Seven allied tanks were now abreast and moving forward, facing six dug-in Russian T-72s. In the background, some three kilometers away, sat a mustard-colored Soviet missile launcher beneath a highway bridge.

They opened fire at 1200 meters.

Commander Hollingberry fired the first salvo, striking the far right tank in the lower turret, causing the steel behemoth to explode. Flames shot forty feet into the air. A 125mm antitank round hit John Boy's Abrams, blasting off his right track and peeling back his armor plate.

"Shoot, goddammit! Shoot!"

A fierce firefight raged back and forth for 60 seconds. John Boy and Cotton both suffered battle damage. Billy got two kills. One of the Challenger tanks had its topside machine gun blown off, plus a huge gouge in the upper turret. Another Challenger was hit, with minor damage. None of the Allied tanks were destroyed, and no personnel were lost.

That was not the fate of the dug-in 72s. All six tanks were wrecked, and all but one of their personnel killed outright or burned to death trying to get out. The commander of the number four Iraqi tank managed to scramble free before his ammunition blew up, incinerating his crew.

Billy signaled Hollingberry who was nearest the bridge. He was down in a blind spot behind a sand embankment. His driver wheeled out into the open. His gunner sighted his 120mm cannon. The Scud driver was backing up, preparing to make a run for it. A single HE

round into the body of the missile was all she wrote. The thing exploded, killing the driver and two missile technicians.

"Skipper, I lost one uh my trainin' wheels."

"Radio the fix-it monkeys. We'll wait around for ya."

"Commander Hollingberry, your boys are real Cracker Jacks®!"

"Yes, indeed. Smashing. What about that poor sod out there?"

"Come on, Cedrick. Let's you an' me get us a live prisoner."

The American captain from Chattanooga, Tennessee, and the
British major from London, England, climbed down from their steel
chariots. Before them stood a defeated Iraqi tank commander with
his hands in the air. He would tell them about the horrors of Saddam
Hussein's murderous regime. Desert Storm lasted three more days;
100,000 Iraqi soldiers would make the ultimate sacrifice.

Chapter Four

Pretty Lola

The Soviet Union collapsed in December of 1991, disintegrating into fifteen separate countries.

Lyndon Johnson, Richard Nixon, and Jimmy Carter had done little to contain the spread of communism. Johnson's Vietnam War policy failed completely. Nixon was saddled with the aftermath. Carter's ignorance of the Soviet Union, expressed by his disappointment and surprise at the Red Army's invasion of Afghanistan, actually helped the spread of the Soviet menace. Ronald Reagan, assisted by Margaret Thatcher, shattered the illusion of détente. President Reagan and his advisors reasoned that the Soviet Union could not sustain a long-term arms race. That is how the US and England eventually bankrupted the Evil Empire.

With the collapse of the Soviet Union, Communist China began its ascension as the supreme leader of the communist world. Many of those who once served the Kremlin switched allegiance to Beijing.

⌒

Lola Lien Hau had purchased an elegant townhouse in Anacostia just south of the Anacostia River. Every morning she would take the 7:20 Metro at the Anacostia station to the L'Enfant Plaza where she transferred to the Orange Line which took her to her Foggy Bottom destination. From the station at Foggy Bottom she often walked to the State Department complex.

Lola was health conscious and quite beautiful. The thirty-three-year old Chinese American was five feet seven inches tall, with jade green eyes, black hair, perky bosoms, a twenty-two inch waist, and a very shapely bottom. She was also a staunch communist, photographing State Department documents for her masters in the Central Planning Committee miles away in Red China.

All her life Lola possessed the innate ability to wrap men around her little finger. She had accomplished that feat with Joseph Carter, her boss, soon after going to work at the State Department. Joseph, married with four children, was smitten with Lola, who was sleeping with him on a regular basis. They even had sex in his private office on occasion. Joseph, in turn, allowed Lola to inspect any records she desired, even though she didn't have the proper security clearance. This had been going on for three and a half years when Mister Carter was informed that Lola Lien Hau was an enemy agent, a spy for Red China. Joseph refused to believe it, although it did give him cause for concern. He informed Lola about the accusations. Lola merely laughed, telling him that someone was jealous of their "special friendship."

⌒

Autumn produced beautiful colors in Anacostia Park.

It was not so pretty in 1932 when 40,000 unemployed World War I veterans gathered in Washington to protest their financial plight brought on by the Great Depression, and an unsympathetic US

Senate. President Hoover ordered the military to disperse the protesters and send them home. But many had no homes to go to following the collapse of Wall Street. General Douglas MacArthur and General George Patton were in charge of removing the veterans. Major Dwight Eisenhower was military liaison with the city police. The debacle which followed led to Franklin Roosevelt's inauguration in 1933.

After taking the oath of office, Franklin delivered his twenty-minute inaugural address, best remembered for his famous words, "So, first of all, let me assert my firm belief that the only thing we have to fear is … fear itself."

Franklin Delano Roosevelt served three terms, dying two months and 24 days into his fourth term as President of the United States. The battle for the Japanese island of Okinawa began April 1, Easter Sunday. It was the bloodiest battle of the Pacific war, lasting 82 days.

President Roosevelt passed away April 12, 1945.

The jogging trail Lola favored led from Anacostia Drive up along the river to East Capitol Street then back to her parked white Corvette. Weather permitting, Lola ran three times a week. The jogging trail meandered through several wooded areas beside the Anacostia River. Up ahead a two-man crew was busy trimming bushes and picking up trash as Lola approached Capitol Street.

The tall one greeted Lola as she approached. "Good afternoon."

Lola didn't speak, turning her head away. She disliked blue collars. They were ignorant and dirty and they smelled bad.

Just as she came abreast of the two men, the shorter one stuck a shovel handle between her feet. Lola tripped and fell. Before she could cry out for help, they dragged her into the underbrush, plunging a hypodermic needle into her neck. The overdose of morphine acted quickly. She struggled briefly, began to lose consciousness, then Lola died.

The men stuffed her body into a garbage barrel on wheels, rolling her back to their pickup truck sitting across the jogging trail in the grass. Ninety minutes later, Lola Lien Hau was on her way to a final rendezvous in the Louisiana bayou with a Cherokee Indian and a retired F-14 fighter pilot.

The twins had just turned eleven. Mama and Daddy and Gran-paw were giving them a birthday party. The young ladies were in the living room with five of their playmates from school. The doorbell rang.

Zephyr and Zelda began jumping up and down when the man who saved them from the KGB intruder walked through the front door. They ran and hugged Cottonmouth, exclaiming their affection for the former Miami detective.

He picked them up, hugging them affectionately. "I miss you little guys. How ya been?"

"We miss you too. We miss you a lot. Why don't you come and live with us?"

"Well, now, I have a wife in Florida. She might get lonely if I up an' left."

"She can come too."

"Here she is. Maybe you better ask her."

Joyce Franklin knelt down between the children. "We can't come and live with you, but you're welcome to come and visit us anytime you like."

"Can we come anytime?"

"Of course, sweetheart. Just ask your mother and father."

The twins scampered off to ask Trudy and Dutch if they could visit the Franklins.

Rico arrived with Marie, Harry and Margot, and Fat Mike and his wife. Sarah and Wayne Compton were present, and Amanda Stone, with her husband, Tony E'Manuel, who was now a brigadier general with the Panamanian Army.

Sarah was delighted to see Amanda. "I'm so happy to see you."

"Me too, girl. Now tell me when are you and Boogie coming to visit?"

"Soon, I promise. We've had our hands full with the marina since Bubba-J died."

"Sell the darn thing. Come stay with us in Panama City. We have a four-bedroom right on the bay. Lots of room. You can walk to everything. Please come. I miss our days as flight attendants. We had so much fun flying."

Allan Ferguson, Winston's friend from Roswell, Georgia, had brought his grandson Mathew to the birthday party. Mathew was twelve years old. The two men had made a lot of money together when Winston was piloting black market goods around North Africa and the Mediterranean. Mister Ferguson had served on PT boats in the Pacific during World War II. They met in Berlin in 1945. Allan and Winston had shared several close calls in the smuggling trades.

They were having a brandy in Winston's library. Everyone else was out in the living room eating, sharing gossip, and enjoying the company. The twins and Mathew were in the backyard playing with the other children. Both girls had a crush on Mathew.

"I know you, Winston. I know you like my own brother. You're into something, I can tell. If there's money to be made, I'd like to get in on it."

"Allan, I'm not going to lie to you. I am involved with something, but it has nothing to do with money. I can't tell you what it is, but I may ask for your help someday. It could be risky."

"Whatever you want my friend. We've traveled a lot of roads together. I'll be around if you need me."

The two old warriors touched glasses and sipped their Napoleon brandy.

The cocktail set in Washington was abuzz with the disappearance of James Cohen and Lola Lien Hau. Everyone knew James Cohen. Lola Lien Hau was not well known, but her disappearance only added fuel to all the gossip. City police found no clues. The Secret Service was baffled. Finally, the FBI was called in.

Had the two run off together? Was foul play involved? Joseph Carter, Lola's employer, claimed to know nothing. The same was true of Cohen's secretary and his coworkers. There simply were no leads, no evidence.

FBI agent Mike Stroud was a hard-nosed former Marine, a senior investigator with twelve years under his belt. The day he interviewed Joseph Carter he knew the man was lying. Guessing correctly that an affair was involved, he threatened Carter with an official visit to question his wife. That was all it took for the State Department employee to break down and spill the beans.

"So you were banging this hot babe, while your loving wife and four kids were sitting at home waiting for Daddy. Is that about the size of it, Mister Goody Two Shoes?"

"Please, you don't understand. Lola is special. I care about her."

"Yeah, you sure as hell do. Now she's gone missing. Did you kill her?"

Carter broke down, sobbing uncontrollably. "No! Please. God, no! I love Lola."

"Well, man up and tell us what you did with the body."

"I swear it. I swear I didn't hurt Lola. If I knew where she was I would help you find her."

"Get this blubbering idiot outta here. He don't know shit from apple butter!"

Mike Stroud sat pondering what Carter had told him. While getting his ashes hauled by Hau, the man had been warned two times that the missing woman was a Red spy. That opened up any number of possibilities. But there was nothing to go on, no leads, no smoking gun, nothing. And Cohen was a complete blank. His sexy girlfriend was dumber than a damn hammer.

Stroud decided to call his contact at CIA headquarters in Langley, Virginia. Ruth Townsend was an old girlfriend from high school. They had remained in touch over the years.

"Ruth, you got anything on those missing people in Washington, Cohen and that Chinese dame?"

"We haven't heard a word, Mike. Did you find any leads?"

"Not a damn thing. Her boss said somebody warned him the Chink was a spy. That's right up your alley. Cohen is a big fat zero. Does the agency know anything about him or this Lola person?"

"All I know is what I read in the newspapers. If we hear anything, I'll call you."

"Thanks, Ruth. I need all the help I can get on this one."

"Take care, my friend. Let's get together for a drink sometime."

As soon as she hung up the telephone, Ruth called George Brown. He arrived at their Langley headquarters an hour later.

"Guess who's on the missing persons' cases in Washington."

"I have no idea."

"Mike Stroud!"

"Hell! That's all we need."

"He has no case so far. We can manipulate him if he picks up the scent."

"Mike is a good man. I'd hate … Well, you know."

"I don't think it'll come to that, George, least ways I hope not. But he is one hell of an investigator."

"I know. I like the guy. This is troubling, to say the least."

"Let's keep this to ourselves for the time being. I don't want Rico and the others worrying."

"I agree. We can salt some false leads if he starts getting close."

"Good idea. I really don't want to harm Michael."

"We knew this might happen. We'll just deal with it as it comes."

"You know, George, I've always admired your commonsense approach. You're a good agent."

"You're a fine woman, Ruth. I count on you, for everything."

"Come on, Mister CIA Man. Let's do Chinese tonight."

Chapter Five

North Tower

A Jimmy Carter appointee at the Pentagon was leaking secret information like a Broadway gossip columnist, both to *The New York Times* and *The Washington Post*, and to a socialist news organization in Geneva, Switzerland. Democrats at the Pentagon and in Congress admired Colonel Franklin Belcore. Republicans liked him as well. He was a responsible appointee in the eyes of most who knew him. What none of them knew or suspected was that he was selling military information to the Russians in Moscow, and had been doing so for six years. Belcore was a devout Bilderberg disciple, believing in One World Government. Nobody knew his secret—except George Brown and Ruth Townsend.

Six months elapsed. Mike Stroud had made no progress on the Cohen and Hau cases. The investigations had turned cold. Stroud was involved now with other cases, but the odd disappearance of the two individuals never left his desk drawer. Every week or so he would pull out the files and read them again.

Brown and Townsend didn't want to stir up another missing persons' controversy, so they set about pursuing a different strategy. Colonel Belcore flew his Learjet to Western Europe every year for his vacation. Being a man of strict protocol, he did this like clockwork on the first day of July. Each vacation, he carried rolls of microfilm that he turned over to a Russian diplomat in Germany. Payment was then transferred into his Swiss bank account. Ruth and George knew his itinerary down to the letter.

July first rolled around, and at precisely 9:00 a.m., Colonel Belcore rolled down a Ronald Reagan runway, destination Hamburg, Germany. His mistress was onboard. They were enjoying a vintage bottle of cognac, 400 miles out at 21,000 feet, when an explosion in the aft compartment sent the plane into a violent nosedive.

"Mayday! Mayday! This is Frank Belcore. Mayday! May—" his radio went silent.

The jet hit the water at over 400 miles an hour. Nothing was left but a fuel slick and chunks of cabin debris when the search plane flew overhead. A Coast Guard cutter arrived, but no bodies were recovered. The plane had burst into a thousand pieces when it hit the sea.

When Mike Stroud heard about the accident, he began adding two and two together. Belcore's distress call was evidence that a catastrophic failure had occurred, but what kind of failure? The whole thing made no sense. James Cohen made no sense. Lola Lien Hau made no sense either. Was there a connection?

"Ruth, I think I'm on to something. I think Cohen and Hau and that Belcore dude are connected. Have you heard anything at all about the colonel or his plane going down?"

"No. We're as much in the dark as you. What do you think it might be?"

"I don't know, but my gut tells me something funny is going on."

"It does sound odd. I'll do some checking and get back to you."

"Okay, Ruth. I'd appreciate anything you come up with."

"Same here, Mike. If you find something, let me know. We'll run it down for you."

When she hung up, George Brown was standing beside her desk. "Well, he's one step closer."

"It's just speculation, George."

"I know."

"You don't sound very convinced."

"I'm not, and neither are you. I can hear it in your voice."

"Damn it, he doesn't know anything."

"Ruth, if he tracks it here, what do you want to do?"

"If it comes to that, I'll take care of it."

"No! If one of us has to do this, it has to be me. I've never said this before. I don't want to upset or embarrass you. But I care about you, Ruth, a great deal. I don't want you involved in an FBI killing."

Ruth Townsend stood up and walked around her desk to confront George. Instead, she placed her arms around his neck, gently pulling him against her, then Ruth Townsend kissed George Brown.

～

"Is this Inspector Stroud?"

"Yeah, who wants to know?"

"This is Doctor Gillespie at Walter Reed Medical Center. We have a patient here asking for you."

"What's his name?"

"Murphy. John Murphy."

"What's Murphy want with me?"

"Mister Murphy says you befriended him once. Says he has information about a Cohen disappearance."

"I'll be there in twenty minutes."

❧

February 26, 1993

A Ryder truck loaded with 1,336 pounds of urea nitrate and several canisters of hydrogen gas was detonated in the bowels of the North Tower of the World Trade Center. Dynamite was used to ignite the fertilizer. It blasted a hole 98 feet across through four parking levels of reinforced concrete, creating a massive crater beneath the explosion. The intent was to topple the North Tower into the South Tower. That failed, although six people were killed and 1,042 injured, mostly during evacuation. Had the rental truck been packed to its 2,000-pound capacity, it might have accomplished the goal sought by the Muslim extremists.

Secret Service agents were called in, and upwards of 700 FBI agents were mobilized worldwide.

Ramzi Yousef, trained in Afghanistan by Al Qaeda, was the mastermind behind the attack. Yousef's uncle, Khalid Sheikh Mohammed, an Al Qaeda operative, gave advice and helped fund the project. Omar Abdel-Rahman, the blind Egyptian cleric in Brooklyn, was also involved and arrested. Six other followers of the Quran participated: Mohammad Salameh, Mahmoud Abouhalima, Ahmed Ajaj, Nidal Ayyad, and Eyad Ismoil. They were eventually captured and given life sentences. Abdul Yasin escaped.

❧

Mike Stroud was on the telephone with Ruth Townsend.

"Them crazy bastards damn near pulled it off."

"I know, I read the report. It's a miracle only six people were killed."

"We know that Yousef asshole is somewhere in the Middle East. We'll find him."

"People like that should be eradicated from the face of the earth."

"Now you're talkin', lady. Those are my sentiments exactly."

"I hope you catch them all."

"Yeah … Dead!"

"Be careful, Mike. Don't get caught doing something you shouldn't."

"Don't worry. I learned all I need to know in the Marines."

"How badly did they damage the Tower?"

"Lots uh cracks, busted pipes, an' stuff, but the foundation held up good."

"I'm glad you're off the case. Let the young ones get their hands dirty."

"Yeah, something like this is good training for 'em."

"Did you ever get a handle on those two men in the alley?"

"Not really. Murphy was asleep in a cardboard box when he heard 'em. The old drunk was too far away to see much. All I got was two guys, one tall with black hair and one medium height with brown hair. He said they grabbed Cohen from behind, did something to him then stuffed 'im in a trunk."

"You think it was a mob hit?"

"Cohen had enemies. He's responsible for that Green Energy thing with China."

"Right. I heard that pissed off a lot of local contractors."

"I dug up something else on the guy. He was associated with a bunch uh commies."

After they hung up, Ruth sat pondering whether Mike was getting a little too close for comfort. If he found out just how deeply Cohen had been involved with those communist elements in Washington, he would be one step closer to her and the organization, especially if Mike tied Cohen and Lola Lien Hau together. Mike was intuitive. He would suspect the CIA was wise to both Cohen and Hau.

Just then she had a chill, as if someone had walked across her grave.

Chapter Six

Doctor Who

London, England

Lydia Sams, MI-6, was down in the Rookery dressed up like an East End prostitute. Her target was a Shia cleric, Mohammad Hussein Farooq. At the mosque where he preached, he taught his followers the way of the true believer: convert, pay tribute, or die. Farooq had recently overseen the murder of a British sailor in the basement of the church. The sailor had been tortured and beaten for hours before they cut off his head while he was still conscious. London police had no clue to his whereabouts. The body had been run through a wood chipper on the outskirts of London.

Uriah Frank, Israeli Mossad, had tracked the cleric from Iran to Paris to England. He and Lydia began their London investigation seven months earlier. Since the cleric's arrival four years ago, five British military personnel had met similar fates. The cleric, smug in his belief he was above British law, railed against England and the Western Powers every time he took the pulpit. Allah demanded obedience. Farooq's seventh-century form of obedience was to force Islam upon the world. If they declined, he would force them to pay tribute as second-class citizens or face the sword. Cleansing the world of infidels was the fanatic's sacred duty in life.

"Hello, Ducky. Give you some nice rumpy-pumpy for 20 quid."

"Get away, you filthy whore."

"Come on, guv'ner. I'll strain yer greens for ya."

"Leave me alone, infidel!"

Lydia grabbed the man's arm, jabbing him with a hatpin she carried hidden in her glove.

"Oww! You slut! Get away from me!"

"Blimey, I've scratched ya with me bracelet."

"I'll have the authorities on you, you degenerate cow!"

Lydia retreated to a doorway and watched. The cleric was a block down Cheshire Street when he felt odd, out of breath. Moments later he was down on the sidewalk, gasping for oxygen. Lydia smiled with satisfaction as the curare took hold. The man died an agonizing death, unable to breath, eyes bulging, slowly suffocating as his paralyzed lungs refused to expand or contract. The cleric's death would be ruled a heart attack.

Lydia crossed the street and got into a waiting MG headed in the opposite direction.

"That won't make up for our lost boys, but it's a start."

"You did well, Lydia. You carried it off splendidly," Uriah said.

Lydia was gazing in the rearview mirror, sponging off her blue eye shadow and black mascara. Her breasts protruded famously from the effects of a push-up bra. Her short red miniskirt partially revealed her black silk panties.

"Fancy some rumpy-pumpy, do ya, ducky?"

He laughed. "Gorgeous as always and twice as deadly."

"Thanks, mate, on both compliments, but what about the rest of those Muslim sods?"

"England has a growing problem, as you well know. Political correctness is allowing them to pour into your country by the thousands. No good will come of that."

"Too many soft-bellied brown tongues in Parliament."

"John Major means well, but he lacks charisma. What England needs is another Winston Churchill."

"Me mum and da used to talk about Sir Winston. He made a grand prime minister, he did."

"I wish Israel had another Golda Meir. Yitzhak Rabin is too liberal for my taste."

"You and I may be a dying breed, Uriah. Too many people want their governments to look after them, tuck them in beddy-bye at night. It's disheartening, to say the least."

"Have you spoken with Ruth Townsend lately?"

"Yes, she's concerned about an FBI investigator who's handling that Cohen case."

"What about it?"

"Ruth says he's very good, that he's picking up bits and pieces here and there."

"What's her opinion?"

"It's troubling. She's conflicted over what to do. I would be too."

"Would you prefer I offer to handle it?"

"No! I need you here, helping me. Rico may be called. I don't envy Ruth."

"It's a hard thing, eliminating one of your own. I've never had to do that."

"We can hope it won't come to that. We'll wait and see."

"Saddam Hussein would make a lovely target."

"Uriah, that's the best idea you've had all bloody week."

The siege of the Branch Davidian compound in Elk, Texas, 9 miles outside Waco, began February 28, 1993. The ATF launched their raid Sunday morning on suspected weapons violations. The raid attempt was poorly managed and quickly deteriorated. A gun battle erupted, four ATF agents and six Branch Davidians were killed. Upon the ATF's failure to secure the compound, the FBI initiated a siege that lasted 51 days.

Attorney General Janet Reno informed President Bill Clinton that David Koresh, who portrayed himself to be the Second Coming of Christ, was sexually abusing the children. Reno stated that any further delay was costing a million dollars a week, and the FBI was tired of waiting. Mass suicide was a possibility. President Clinton told her to do whatever she considered prudent. The final assault took place April 19, 1993. Later on it was asserted that the FBI supplied Reno and Clinton with false information. Who said what is unclear, as much of what was said remains classified.

During the siege, a number of religious scholars attempted to persuade the FBI that the Branch Davidians, who believed Armageddon was at hand, might misinterpret the FBI actions as having biblical significance. That would likely increase the chances of a violent and deadly confrontation.

Meanwhile, the FBI had shot out the water towers on top of the compound and cut off the electricity. Bradley Fighting Vehicles were used to smash down the fences and run over automobiles. Fifty caliber rifles and 40mm grenade launchers were employed. The M-79s fired tear gas canisters and flash grenades. Noise was broadcast over loud speakers at night to cause sleep deprivation. Finally, armored CEVs with long steel booms were used to punch holes in the walls of the buildings. Fires broke out. Seventy-six people were burned to death, including twenty-three children.

Mike Stroud was on the telephone with Ruth Townsend. "Have you ever seen an ATF agent?"

"No, I haven't"

"I was in a gas station in Alcoa, Tennessee, about two years ago. Three ATF agents came in, one so fat you couldn't see his belt buckle. The other two looked like they just stepped out of *Deliverance*. Every one of them carried an Army .45. That's what we have in the ATF today."

"No wonder it started out badly."

"No wonder, my ass. Those clowns couldn't field a weenie roast!"

"Stay clear, Mike. It can only damage your career."

"I'm cool. I'm keeping records on the big boys."

"That's good. If something else goes wrong, the higher-ups, including Sessions, will be looking for a scapegoat."

"They won't get me. I have dossiers on most of them. Some are real jewels."

"I can just imagine."

"I heard you and Mister Brown are an item now."

"Damn, Mike, you sure do get around."

"Is it true?"

"Yes, John and I are getting married."

"Looks like I'm a day late an' a dollar short. I was gonna ask you out again, but since you're spoken for I'd be honored to come to the wedding."

"I'm flattered, Mike. You're a sweetheart. I'll let you know."

"Waco was a fucking disaster."

"Yes, from what we've heard, Reno and those field agents really blew it."

"In spades! Reno fell for a line of bullshit."

"You mean they lied?"

"Some did. They wanted to show off their military toys."

"And seventy-six people died?"

"Fried is a better word."

"That's a horrible way to die."

"Yeah! Now they're all running for cover. We were just following orders, blah-blah-blah."

"Following orders, my ass! It sounds like they murdered those poor people."

"They probably did."

"Don't trust the government, Mike. There's a lot of stuff going on behind closed doors."

"You said it!"

"Any new developments on Cohen and Hau?"

"I have a few leads."

"Can you share them with me?"

"I'll let ya know. Oh, yeah. I just found out Hau was a Chinese spy."

Ruth hung up. Mike was getting close.

⌁

The 1994 inflation rate was 2.61%. Dow Jones average was $3,834, while interest rates held steady at 8.5%. Cost of a new home was around $119,000. The average income was $37,000, and a gallon of gasoline cost $1.09. A loaf of bread was $1.59, and a dozen eggs were 86 cents. The twins were twelve years old and attending seventh grade. They were beginning to blossom like their mother, budding breasts and cute bottoms, which all the boys noticed and appreciated.

Zelda was expressing her feelings to Mathew and Zephyr about a new song she liked. They were in the backyard. Allan Ferguson and Winston Peters were in the house watching the Atlanta Falcons game with the Washington Redskins.

"It's called "Zombie." This girl sings it. It's something about soldiers and stuff. It's really good, but I don't understand it."

"I heard it on the radio and I didn't get it either, so I asked Grandfather. He said it was about Ireland and England back in 1916.

They were fighting each other, and people were getting killed," Mathew explained."

Zephyr asked him, "Do you ever watch *Beavis and Butthead*?"

"Oh, wow. Those guys are crazy. I watch it with my dad sometimes."

"Gran-paw thinks O J Simpson killed his wife."

"I think so too. He just looks creepy."

"I think he's handsome."

"Maybe he'll just cut off your nose and a big toe."

"Yuck! No way!"

Zelda asked Mathew another question. "Did you like *Forrest Gump*?"

"Bubba Gump Shrimp!"

The twins giggled.

"My favorite is *Doctor Who*," Mathew shared.

Zelda spoke up. "Oh, me too! I love his scarf."

Zephyr continued. "I did a school report on *Doctor Who*. He's a Time Lord who travels in time and space in his TARDIS. When he gets old or hurt he can regenerate his body. Sarah Jane Smith is his girlfriend. And he has a robot dog named K-9."

"Do you think we'll travel in time and space like Captain Kirk?"

"Yeah, and probably get captured by Ming the Merciless."

"Snow White would save us."

"What about Wolverine or Captain America?"

"That would be cool."

"Did you see *The Lion King*?"

"No, did you?

"It's playing at the Buckhead. Let's go see it."

The kids ran into the house to ask if they could go to the show.

Twenty minutes later they were on their way. A quarter mile down West Paces Ferry, they turned left on Roswell Road and walked to the theater. By the time they were seated with their popcorn and Orange Crush, the feature was just beginning.

The Atlanta Falcons won the football game 27 to 20.

Chapter Seven

The Shadow Party

Two years elapsed. Zelda and Zephyr were fourteen, and Mathew had just turned fifteen. Zelda had beaten out a whole field of girls who wanted to become cheerleaders. Zephyr was fast becoming the brain of the Henry family. She was studying mathematics and physics as a freshman in high school. Zelda was more interested in cheerleading and football. Zephyr was interested in obtaining a PhD someday.

"We're playing the Vikings Friday night. Is Gran-paw still coming?"

"Mom and Dad are too. Gran-paw's more interested in your cheerleading than football."

"I'll do my flips for Gran-paw."

"You know, Zelda, I'm proud of you."

"That's the nicest thing you ever said to me."

"I mean it, girl. You've got what it takes. Cheerleading and football don't really interest me, but you like it and that's what's important. Every person should follow their own heart."

"Why so serious tonight?"

"I don't know. It just feels right."

"I'm glad we're sisters. Sometimes I feel like I know what you're thinking. It's just a feeling I get, but it scares me a little."

"That's what I mean. I can feel your energy."

"We never talked like this before."

"It's nice, isn't it?"

"Yes, very nice. Do you think we're getting like those twins who know each other's thoughts?"

"Maybe not exactly, but something like that."

"I wish I was smart like you, Zephyr."

"You're plenty smart. Just learn to trust your instincts."

Trudy yelled to them from the kitchen. "Soup's on. Come and get it. "

Zephyr hugged Zelda. Zelda hugged her back.

"Being twins is really cool."

⸺

A week later Dutch drove the family to their favorite restaurant over in Vinings, Georgia. It was catfish night, and the twins were starving.

Winston teased Zelda. "You got enough hush puppies there to float down the Chattahoochee."

"They're good, Gran-paw. Try one."

"Umm, this is good."

The twins had been comparing experiences that they originally thought were coincidence. They were excited about their newly discovered clairvoyant capabilities. Tonight they had chosen to share it with Gran-paw and their parents.

"We have a secret."

"What's that, dear?"

"We can tell what the other is thinking."

Dutch turned to look at his daughters. So did Trudy. Winston just smiled. He'd known for a year, but had elected to remain silent until they figured it out for themselves.

Trudy questioned Zephyr. "How can you possibly know that?"

"When Zelda is happy or sad or just thinking about something, I can sense her thoughts, or I feel the way she feels. We've been talking about it. She said the same thing about me. It's kinda weird, Mom, but we love it."

"When Zephyr fell off her bicycle and skinned her knee, I got a pain in my knee. I didn't think about it much. Then when she got mad at a boy who was teasing her in school, I got upset too and I didn't know why. I wasn't even there."

Winston chimed in. "I've known they were like this, but I wanted them to find out for themselves. We have a very special pair of young ladies here."

Dutch finally found his voice. "This is amazing. I've heard of such things, but this is just amazing."

"Dutch and I do good work." Trudy smiled.

Everyone laughed. An awakening had begun.

⌒

TWA Flight 800 exploded in midair and crashed into the Atlantic Ocean twelve minutes after takeoff from the John F Kennedy Airport, July 17, 1996. All 230 passengers and crew onboard were killed. Witnesses on boats in the vicinity reported seeing a streak of light ascending from the sea. Two fireballs were then observed falling from the sky. It was believed the 747 broke apart.

Ruth Townsend and George Brown were having dinner at Tim's Crab House in Quantico, Virginia. They'd driven down the night before and rented a cabin on the beach for the weekend. The two CIA agents had worked together for years before finally admitting they loved one another.

"Mike Stroud thinks it's a cover-up. He said 78 agents investigated the explosion, interviewing 38 witnesses who were out in boats. Some saw a white light go up. Mike believes it was a missile. The FBI dug up records on rented boats that night. Radar detected a blip merging with the aircraft."

"Then why cover it up?"

"Mike believes it comes from the White House."

"So it's politics as usual?"

"Politics, oil, arrogance, and bullshit."

"Could the FBI be wrong?"

"That's a possibility. They blew it at Ruby Ridge and Waco."

"I know Mike's your friend, Ruth. What are we going to do?"

"He's connected Cohen and those other two. What do you think?"

"Do you believe we could turn him?"

"I don't know. He's a straight arrow."

"If we can't, we have to tell Rico."

"That bothers me. I don't want to hurt Michael."

"Let's call Winston and see what he thinks."

"Good idea. I'll call Monday morning."

"What do you think about this 747 business?"

"My guess would be Muslims. Those people are nuts."

"It hard to believe a so-called religion wants to kill everybody."

"That Mohammad bastard must have been a real beauty."

"Right! Too bad somebody didn't clobber his ass way back when."

"What about our wedding, George?"

"Well, we could have it in September. The leaves are changing then."

"I like that … with a few of our friends at Arlington?"

"Yes, up there where they do the Changing of the Guard."

"They'll remember that one, won't they?"

"They'll remember you, pretty lady."

"I want Winston and Rico to be there."

"And John Franklin and his wife. I respect that man."

"How'd you like him and Rico coming after you?"

"I think I'd take out some extra insurance, sweetheart."

"They're about as good as it gets, aren't they?"

"John, especially. He has that look about him."

"I'm so happy. I never knew it could be like this."

"Me too. Why did we wait so long?"

"Our jobs, and the fear of making fools of ourselves."

"I like being your fool."

"I love you, Mister Fool!"

"No matter what happens, I'll do whatever it takes to protect you."

"I know, baby. Why don't you take me back to our place and protect me some more tonight?"

"Think I should eat a few extra oysters?"

"You better eat a whole plateful."

George smiled—and signaled the waiter.

❧

Mike Stroud unlocked his front door, walked in, and flipped on a light switch.

"Two fingers, Mike, left hand. Toss your gun over there on the rug."

He did as he was told. "I thought it would be George or one of your Mafia pals."

"So you knew."

"Not exactly, but I figured you were in on it."

Ruth Townsend motioned with the .357 she held in her hand. "Sit down over there on the sofa."

Mike sat down on his sofa. "You here to kill me?"

"I have a proposition for you."

"Money, sex? What is it?"

"Nothing so crude, Michael."

"Yeah, right."

"Several years ago George and I discovered a shadow government working inside our Federal Government, right here in Washington. Since then it's grown. Now we have people in Congress and different agencies working to change our republic into a socialist regime, like France or Italy."

"That gives you no right to kill people."

"You've killed before. What gave you the right?"

"I … uh … I'm FBI!"

"You were a Marine too."

"I'll always be a Marine."

"And on both counts you swore to uphold the Constitution and protect the United States of America, did you not?"

"You're trying to put words in my mouth."

"Did you or didn't you, goddammit?"

Mike sensed he'd better answer truthfully. He'd never seen this side of Ruth before. "Yes, I did, both times."

"Our republic in under attack by left-wing zealots and impressionable fools. Is that part of the pledge, or do we just sweep it under the rug?"

"Dammit, Ruth, you're twisting my words."

"Twisting, hell! Do you love this country or not?"

"I love Miss Liberty, bearing her torch and tabula ansata out there in New York Harbor."

"Well said, Mike. I'm impressed."

"So what the hell do you want from me?"

"Join us."

"And go around killing people?"

"Not people, Mike. Traitors! Men and women beyond the reach of the law."

"Sounds like half uh Washington."

"Just the worst ones, Mike."

"This is crazy. The CIA and God knows who going around whacking American citizens."

"Cohen was a scumbag, funding the Communist Party right here in the capitol. Lola Lien Hau was a Chinese spy, stealing secrets from the State Department for Peking. That Belcore asshole with the Pentagon was selling microfilm to the Russians. There were others you don't know about. None of them would ever have served a single day in prison. They had the funds and the connections to escape justice."

"How many others?"

"You don't need to know that."

"If I get caught they'll strap me down in the electric chair or hang my ass."

"As a Marine, would you lay down your life for your country?"

"You know I would. That's not fair."

"Is it fair that these individuals betrayed their country?"

"Damn! You're one hell of an interrogator."

"Does it make sense or not, Mike."

"Okay, it makes sense. Who you want me to kill?"

"Don't be facetious, Mike. We don't want you to kill anybody. Just keep quiet about my people."

"You're asking an awful lot of me."

"And don't whine. It's unbecoming of you."

"Ruth, if it weren't for George I'd marry you myself, if you'd have me."

"That is a lovely compliment. If I didn't love George, I might take you up on your invitation."

Ruth laid her weapon on the table beside her chair. "Pick up your gun, Mike."

"You gonna shoot me in self-defense?"

"Pick up your weapon."

Mike Stroud walked over, leaned down, and hefted his .45. When he turned around Ruth Townsend was calmly sitting in her chair, her

.357 still on the table beside her. He studied her for several moments, made a decision, and then tossed his automatic down on the couch.

"You win."

"Thank you, Michael."

"I meant what I said about you and George."

"I know. I remember prom night when we made love in the backseat of your old Chevy."

"You won't have to jimmy the door again. There's a key under a rock by that azalea bush out front."

"I want you to come to our wedding."

"I'll be there, wishing it was me."

Ruth retrieved her revolver, walked over to Mike and kissed him, then she walked out the front door.

⌁

"You took care of it, how?"

"Let's just say that Mike is a true patriot and a loyal Marine."

"You beat all, Ruth. I got the best when I got you."

"And I got the best with you, Mister Brown."

"Can you tell me about it?"

"That's a part of my life I wish to keep to myself."

"I know you care about Michael. I won't ask again."

"Thank you, George."

"Could we ask for his help if we needed it?"

"Yes, I'm sure of it. But I don't want him involved in any of the killing."

"I understand. We've placed enough burden on him already."

"Yes, knowing about us is more than enough."

"Where do you want to eat tonight?"

"We could go over to Georgetown and stroll down Wisconsin. We'll find something."

"Good suggestion. Get your coat and let's go.

It was a lovely summer evening. Fall was just around the corner—and the union of a man and woman very much in love.

Chapter Eight

Carnivore

John Franklin and Joyce were next door visiting with Katherine and John Parker. Cotton had streaks of gray now while John was almost white. The women were both attractive and still retained their girlish figures. John sometimes carried his damaged arm in a neck sling. His nightmares about Vietnam had left him for the most part. Once in a while the battle on the mountain where Steve was killed came back, but Katherine was always there to hold John when he awoke. Joyce had since recovered from Steve's death, and dearly loved her new husband. The two neighbors had become the best of friends.

"How's the little one?" Joyce asked.

"Jonathan is five now, and a handful just like his mother was," Katherine replied.

"Samantha sure is a purty gal. Roger's a lucky fella," Cottonmouth said.

Joyce added, "You know, when Steve got killed my world ended.

John has given me a new life. And Sam and the baby are just like angels. I can't tell you how much I love them, and my wonderful Roger."

"Roger's a good father," Katherine said. "He does things with that little boy all the time."

"You heard from Rico lately?" John Parker asked.

"Rico's cool. We stay in touch," Cottonmouth replied.

"I'll never forget our shootout on Dixie Highway. I still think about it sometimes. I'm sorry McCoy got killed."

"Bill was a good egg. I miss my partner."

"I miss Steve too. I guess that never goes away."

"Yeah, but we're still here. That's what counts, you an' Kat, me an' Joyce."

Katherine and Joyce were out in the kitchen preparing cocktails.

Katherine was teasing Joyce. "He's so big. How do you do it?"

"He is big, real big. And I love it!"

Katherine cackled out loud. "Joyce, you won't do. I just love you."

"We're lucky, you and I. We have two good men and a great life."

"Remember when Rico hid us in that airport in New Orleans? I was scared to death over John."

"I was too, but you were such a mess that you kept me busy."

"Joyce, you're the best friend a girl could ever have."

"And didn't we have fun at that resort? We both got sideways."

"That was fun. Let's take the boys their drinks."

Back in the living room John had a fire going in the fireplace.

"Looks like Clinton's gonna take it again."

"I like ole Bill, but that Al Gore's a real asshole. You ever hear him talk?"

"I heard him once. That was enough."

"Them Seminoles mopped the field with our ass first quarter. The paper said Wuerffel got knocked down 32 times. But we still got a shot, if Danny can hang in there."

"Tennessee was a big surprise. I thought they might beat us. We scored 35 points before they knew what hit 'em."

"Let's hope Arizona State gets knocked off like those Tennessee boys."

"Yeah, and our Gators go on to the Sugar Bowl."

"Time to eat, guys."

Moses Blue Pony was waiting on his front porch for Karl Musgrove to arrive. Another package was en route. White Devil and the blind cocker spaniel were wagging their tails back and forth on the wooden flooring. Swamp Kat sat on the top step beside her master. They knew company was coming.

Karl pulled up in his pickup truck and got out. "Moses, we got another one."

"What you bring me?"

"Russian, big shot, dope dealer."

"I'll make fire."

They stripped the body of gold chains, rings, watch, and belt, then burned his shoes, wallet, and clothing. The Russian was big. It took both of them to drag the body to the bass boat.

"This bastard must weight 220 or 230. Your alligator will get his fill tonight."

"Maybe we buy him refrigerator for leftovers."

Karl laughed. "You are one crazy redskin."

"Sure, ever' body crazy after Vietnam."

"Ya know, in a way I miss it."

"Me too. We both nuts."

"They say this dead fuck killed fifty people."

"Him crazy too!"

"They got 'im in Little Rock. Said he had over $200,000 in his Mercedes. They brought us another pokeful."

"Back yard getting like bank."

"I wish we could invest some without the Feds finding out. Buy some real estate someplace, or some gold, maybe."

"Good idea, but how?"

"I don't know. I'll ask a friend of mine who's a financial adviser."

Moses drove the bass boat out through the swamp until they came to a small island where the alligator lived. There he lay, up on a mossy bank sunning his long, scaly body. At their approach, the alligator lifted his head.

"I swear that is the biggest alligator I ever saw."

"Him maybe fourteen feet, 900 pounds."

"That's a lot uh whoop-ass."

They struggled getting the Russian over the side without tipping the boat over. Moses paddled back a few yards. The giant reptile slid down into the water.

Back at the cabin they counted out their money.

"Thirty thousand ain't too bad for two ole country boys."

"I get Mason jar."

They stuffed 300 one hundred dollar bills in a quart jar then Blue Pony sealed the metal lid with candle wax. They placed it in a plastic bag, taped it shut, and buried it in the back yard beside the rose bushes. Moses' favorite was white American Beauties.

"I been thinkin', Mose. Those metal lids might rust, even taped up. We better come up with a better way to hide our money. I'll check at the hardware store and see what they got."

"Good idea. Money get wet, rot like paper."

"Someday we oughta move away from here. South America, maybe, Australia, maybe even Vietnam. They like Americans in Vietnam. Argentina, lots uh places. We could live like kings."

"I take my animals?"

"Sure, we could buy some uh those cage things in town."

"Good idea. Someday people who kill assholes get caught. Then bad news."

"Yeah, we don't want to be around when the shit hits the fan."

"Maybe find me uh wife."

"Or a pretty girlfriend. You're good-lookin', Mose. Women will cream their jeans over you."

"How much money we got?"

"Better than $300,000. We need half a mil before we bug out."

"Mister Alligator get fat."

"I figure about three more years."

Chapter Nine

Short Sale

The year 1997 was the beginning of President Clinton's second term. O.J. Simpson beat the murder rap, but was judged liable in a civil suit. China's Deng Xiaoping died at 92. Israel approved expansion of her Jewish settlements into East Jerusalem, provoking further unrest in the Middle East. A third of Albania's population lost their life savings in a series of pyramid schemes, riots followed. The Hale-Bopp comet sailed past the earth. And Tiger Woods won his first major championship at the Masters Golf Tournament in Athens, Georgia.

Congress voted a number of major tax cuts to stimulate the US economy. Hong Kong reverted back to Chinese rule. Then Versace was shot dead on the front steps of his Miami villa. The Clinton White House and the GOP agreed on measures to balance the federal budget. Princess Diana, 36, was killed in a Paris automobile accident. Mother Teresa passed away at age 87. Taliban leaders seized Kabul, Afghanistan, initiating a strict adherence to the Quran. Public floggings, stoning, and cutting off the heads of Christians and nonbelievers followed. Islamic militants murdered 62 people at the Luxor tourist center in Egypt.

The FBI ended a 16-month investigation into TWA Flight 800, stating that no foul play was suspected. And a Paris court convicted "Carlos the Jackal," a Venezuelan communist terrorist, of murder.

The Shadow Party was growing.

Short selling is the sale of a security not actually owned by the seller. The seller, in effect, borrows the security's ownership. An escrow account is set up with the seller's purchase price, plus a maintenance percentage of the purchase price, in the escrow account. Short selling is motivated by the belief that a security's price will decline, enabling the stock or bank note to be purchased back at a lower price, thus enabling a short sale profit. The difference between the purchase price and the selling price dictates any profit or loss.

George Soros shorted the British pound in 1992 which had been placed in a precarious position due to England's desire to buoy its currency artificially through the ERM, European Exchange Rate Mechanism. The idea was to keep its currency value above 2.7 marks to the pound. That was unwise due to England's low interest rates and high inflation ratio. It was fundamentally unsound because Britain's inflation rate was many times that of Germany's. George Soros and several others saw the handwriting on the wall. They shorted the British pound, selling the currency while promising to buy it back at a future date. England was losing money hand over fist, so she withdrew from the ERM. The pound plummeted and Soros bought the pounds back, thus pocketing the difference between one and two billion dollars.

Soros did the same thing again in 1997 against the Thai baht and the Malaysian ringgit, causing those currencies to crash. It was reported that Soros siphoned off billions from the government of Thailand and her population. The man is an 85-year-old Hungarian-American Jew with no allegiance to Israel or the United States. He believes himself a messianic figure whose utopian vision of "Open Society" is the elixir for world peace. Some call him the master manipulator of hit-and-run capitalism.

Karl Popper's Open Society envisioned no borders, no individual identity, and no religion. Soros toppled the Czech Republic, Yugoslavia, and the government of Georgia. He achieved that through bribery, blackmail, control of the media, voter fraud, phony polls, and paid street demonstrations. He and a handful of speculators looted the budding democracy in Russia, causing that economy to collapse back into the arms of a communist dictatorship. Poland was another victim of George Soros.

Soros is associated with the Rothschilds and their powerful allies who are believed to be the power behind Soros. That includes circles of the British oligarchy, and the "hot money" gang in Israel. The American Federal Reserve is suspected of being involved. David Rockefeller's Trilateral Commission is thought to be a player. Another group with its hands in the till is the Bilderberg Group. Soros is a member of the Bilderberg Group.

One World Government is their ultimate goal. Destruction of the United States as a superpower is crucial so America can no longer stand in the way of Big Brother. Soros is one of the prime movers, subverting traditional societies to fit his Open Society. He brings down governments by subversion, moral decay, and revolution through his financial patronage via the usual suspects: socialism, communism, and violence.

Soros funds a myriad of organizations in the United States: The Center for American Progress, MoveOn.Org, American Votes, America Coming Together, Media Matters, Politico, MSNBC, The Thunder Road Group, NOW, and the SEIU. Additional affiliates include the ACLU, Sierra Club, People for the American Way, NAACP,

National Education Association, The Human Rights Campaign, AFL-CIO, Emily's List, Data Warehouse, Planned Parenthood, ACORN, Common Cause, and the Association of Trial Lawyers of America. There are dozens more.

George Soros is the financial power behind the Shadow Party inside the American Federal Government. The United Nations is their intended seat of authority for One World Government. The above secret societies are the intended puppet masters.

⌒

"That son of a bitch is a shill, a front man for a bunch of elites bent on ruling the world."

"How do you know that?"

"A friend at Scotland Yard sent me his dossier."

"Damn, Ruth, you know everybody."

"Be careful, Mike. Those people can make you disappear with no questions asked."

"I hear ya, lady."

"We debated going after Soros, but he's just one in hundreds, maybe thousands."

"That would be difficult. He's surrounded himself with some serious security."

"It could be done with a rifle or an IED, but they'd find us sooner or later."

"High profile means high risk."

"Yes, a million dollars for us is nothing more than chump change for them."

"What do you plan to do?"

"Same thing we've been doing. It eliminates some of the worst ones."

"If I can be of help, let me know. I can search the files for you."

"I appreciate that, Mike. I may need you someday."

"I hope you're happy, Ruth. That wedding was a peach."

"Yes, it was wonderful, wasn't it?"

"I like your husband … the dirty rat!"

"You silly thing. He likes you too."

"Listen, I'll rustle up a date some night, and we'll all go out for dinner."

"That would be nice. I'll tell George."

"Okay, let me know when. There's a redhead in the office been giving me the eye."

"Lucky girl."

"Oh, mama!"

"You're a mess. Take care. I gotta get some work done."

"See ya."

Ruth sat at her desk staring out the window at the Potomac River. Things were getting worse. More and more people were climbing on the George Soros bandwagon. What could they be thinking? The future of the American Republic was in jeopardy, but all they seemed to care about was their next paycheck and receiving invitations to the best dinner parties. The fabric of American society was coming undone.

෴

Billy Ray Donavan was Karl Musgrove's nephew. His mother had married a lay preacher who got her pregnant then ran off with a striptease dancer. His father, the preacher, wound up in a Texas prison. Billy Ray had gone to visit his father one time. He never went back. The preacher turned out to be a garden variety con artist.

Billy was lodged in a motel room on the outskirts of Hattiesburg, Mississippi. His girlfriend was still in bed, asleep. Billy Ray was on leave. So was Wanda Jean McBride. She and Billy Ray had met during Desert Storm. Wanda Jean was an Apache helicopter pilot. She had knocked out three Iraqi trucks and a T-72 Russian tank during the battle. Billy

Ray was in love. So was Wanda Jean. They planned to marry and set up housekeeping in Chattanooga after being discharged from the Army.

Wanda opened her eyes, gazing over at Billy Ray sitting at a desk writing his mother a letter.

"Hey there, hot stuff."

"Hey there, yourself. You awake?"

"Yes, want some breakfast?"

"Sure, there's a Waffle House down the street."

"I'll shower then we'll go."

Wanda climbed out of bed, naked. Billy loved looking at her. Wanda was tall with the physique of an athlete. She had black hair, hazel eyes, full sensual lips, supple breasts, round muscular buttocks, and long beautiful legs. She had come in third on the obstacle course during basic training. Wanda Jean was an excellent pilot and a dedicated soldier.

At breakfast, Billy Ray posed a question to Wanda. "You wanna stay in the Army?"

"Why don't we sign up for one more tour? We'd get a big bonus."

"I like that bonus idea. But what if we get separated?"

"If we get married, the Army will station us at the same base, unless there's another war."

"Then let's do it, babe. We got five days left. We can drive down to Slidell. My uncle lives there."

"Oh, Billy Ray, you wonderful man. You're too much."

"We can pack up and leave right after breakfast."

"Okay, let's do it."

"I'll call ahead and tell him we're coming. Mom is sick. I'll call her, and you two can talk."

The drive to Slidell took an hour and thirty-five minutes. They located Karl in a gated condominium complex five miles east of the city. His place was decorated with war mementos from his two tours of duty in Vietnam. There were pictures of his squadron mates and the

F-14 he flew. Karl's war medals were on display in a glass case. There was a framed photo of a man in battle fatigues above the case.

"You folks want a drink?"

"We'd love one."

Karl fixed three Bloody Marys.

"I got a preacher buddy who can perform the ceremony."

"That would be great."

'When you want to do it?"

"Tomorrow, if we can."

Karl got on the phone and called the pastor. "He said okay, one o'clock at the church."

Wanda jumped up and hugged Karl.

"There's a friend I want to invite."

"Sure, who is it?"

"He's a Cherokee. We were in 'Nam together."

At the Presbyterian Church, Karl Musgrove gave away the bride. Moses Blue Pony was the ring bearer. Wanda Jean and Billy Ray were all smiles. After the ceremony, Moses handed Wanda an Indian charm, a little jade turtle.

Wanda was taken with the pretty charm. "I'll cherish this always. Thank you so much, Mister Blue Pony."

"You take care of Mister Turtle. Him powerful medicine."

It was then Billy Ray recognized Moses. "Say, you're that guy in the picture."

Karl smiled. "When I got shot down, Mose and his squad found me. I was hurt pretty bad. They saved my life."

"You never told me that before."

"I never told you a lot of things about Vietnam. It's best forgotten. Now, let's go someplace and celebrate. You two deserve some champagne."

At the restaurant on Highway 190 they were seated at a rear table near the kitchen. The waitress had just brought out a chilled bottle of

Charles Heidsieck Brut Reserve, four servings of red cabbage and apple salad, and a platter of Bubba's Famous Mudbugs.

An obnoxious drunk appeared from the bar area, 6' 1", 225 pounds of pure redneck badass. He leaned down on the tabletop, informing Wanda Jean she was "a purty lookin' piece uh ass."

Before anyone could speak Moses Blue Pony bolted from his seat, chopping the edge of his hand into the man's throat. The man crashed to the floor, gasping for breath. Moses straddled the man's stomach, holding his jaw with his left hand, producing a knife with his right, which he inserted partway up one nostril of Mister Badass. A trickle of blood ran down his chin.

"Open mouth again, I scalp nose!"

The terrified man stared at Blue Pony, afraid to move. Management came over, separated the two, and threw out the drunk. They apologized for the intrusion, informing Karl the meal was on the house.

Billy Ray shook his head in amazement. "Damn, Moses, I'd hate to have you pissed off at me."

Wanda, still wide-eyed, responded, "You're a one-man army, Mister Blue Pony. You coulda won Desert Storm all by yourself."

"Many bad memories from war."

"Listen, guys. You ever need anything, me and Wanda will be there for ya."

Karl patted Billy on the shoulder. "You got a good woman there, son. Take good care of her."

"I will, Karl. I damn sure will."

Wanda stood up, leaned across the table, and kissed Moses on the cheek. That was the first time Karl Musgrove had ever seen Moses Blue Pony blush.

⌇

"They're digging tunnels. But it's a wide area so we seldom spot one from the air," Uriah said.

"You mean those camel shaggers are coming in underground?" Lydia asked.

"Yes, we lost a soldier last month when he walked across a hidden entrance and the trapdoor fell in. They killed him. My people could hear them inside."

"What happened?"

"They got the body out. Two more soldiers got hurt doing that. Then they drove a fuel truck up and dumped four hundred gallons of gasoline down the entrance. A soldier tossed in a grenade. Two hundred yards back into Palestine camouflaged air holes blew fire in the air. I wish I'd been there to see that."

"Shish ke-bob did originate in the Middle East, ya know."

"What people don't understand, Lydia, is that Palestine sits right in the middle of the State of Israel. When the UN partitioned Israel in 1947, they should have placed Palestine at one end or the other. Instead, what they did was mix the Arabs and Jews together."

"Indeed, they buggered the whole beastly affair."

"Exactly, and Jerusalem sits right in the middle of Palestine."

"I don't envy your people, Uriah."

"If England doesn't stop her wholesale immigration of Muslims, you're going to have the same thing in London in a few years."

"The world is run by troglodytes and idiots. Blighty is no different."

"What's the latest on our Langley friends?"

"Remember that FBI man Ruth was fretting over so?"

"Yes."

"He came over to our side."

"Danken Gott!"

"And Ruth Townsend married George Brown."

"Excellent!"

"Now, how are we going to deal with this Dunbar chap and his gang of cutthroats?"

"I've been thinking. Dunbar has another shipment going out

Friday. We know he'll be onboard to collect from his buyers. What if the ship never makes port?"

"How might we pull that off?"

"Most of the crew will be in the pubs and whorehouses until the day they sail. We need a distraction to get onboard and plant a bomb in the arms locker."

"Good thinking! A timing device until they're well out to sea. But what kind of distraction?"

"I haven't worked that out yet."

"What about a fire?"

"Too dangerous. We might burn up the wharf."

"How 'bout a punch-up?"

"A what?"

"Spread rumors, insight a bloody riot."

"That might work, but we only have three days to do this."

"You're right. Let me think a mo."

Lydia cogitated while Uriah sipped his Regent's Punch.

"What if I dress up like a tart and do me thing in front of the crew?"

"Good God, Lydia, you're liable to get raped."

"Hmmm, I never thought of that."

"But if you were in a boat, they couldn't get at you!"

"Blimey! And you'd have access to the gangplank. I'll turn their crank with me strawberry creams."

Two days later they were ready. Lydia had rented a 22-foot motor launch, and Uriah had built a C-4 bomb to resemble a lunchpail. They set out at nine in the morning while there was still fog along the waterfront. On the *Al Qattara* only a skeleton crew was aboard.

"Ahoy there, mates. Fancy a little having it off, do ya?

"Jesus, look down there!"

"*Wald el hawat!* She's got 'er tits out."

"Go tell the others!"

"Shag me backdoor, sailor boys. It's me twenty-quid special!"

Lydia bent over with her blue panties showing, wiggling her shapely bottom suggestively for her captive audience.

"*Nekni ana sharyaana!*"

Uriah walked up the gangplank carrying his lunchpail. No one paid him any attention. They were all hanging over the port railing. He located the bulkhead hatch, and went inside. Going down the stairwell, he encountered a man coming up.

"Who're you?"

"Maintenance. I'm here to inspect the diesel engine."

"All right, get on with it.'"

Uriah found the door to the arms locker. Using a locksmith tool, he soon had it open. At the back of the room he discovered crates of C-4 and TNT. There were stacked boxes of mortar rounds, beehive shells, machine guns and rifles, grenades, tons of weapons and munitions. Uriah flipped a tiny lever then concealed his lunchpail among the explosives.

"Who the hell are you?"

"I wanna buy me one uh them guns."

"How'd you get in here?"

"Tha door wadn't locked."

The man eyed him suspiciously, resting his right hand on the butt of a revolver. Uriah looked down at the floor, avoiding the man's eyes, shoving his hands in his pockets in mock embarrassment. Uriah fingered a five-inch switchblade.

"Well, get the hell out! They ain't for sale!"

Uriah made his way back up the stairwell. Topside the men were still at the port railing, cheering and grabbing their crotches amid boisterous yelling and laughter.

"Look me up at the Blue Moon, seadogs. I'll toss yer greens for ya, I will."

Uriah hurried down the gangplank and disappeared into the fog.

The Daily Telegraph broke the story.

"The freighter *Al Qattara*, bound for Syria, has been lost in the Mediterranean Sea. A massive explosion was witnessed by ships miles away. The cause of the disaster remains unknown. No survivors were found. Arms dealer Marcus Dunbar, owner of the ship, is believed to have been onboard. A maritime investigation continues."

Chapter Ten

Zelda

Zephyr opened her eyes. The room was almost dark. A window at the top of a high wall with burglar bars cast a rectangle of light across the room against the opposite wall. The room smelled dank and musty. Her cheeks burned where the chloroform had been held against her face. She was lying on a concrete floor. Zelda lay beside her, unconscious.

Fear took hold. She remembered two men walking up and grabbing her and Zelda. They spoke in a foreign language. She fought to get away, fought hard, but the rag he held over her face was the last thing she remembered.

Zelda was facedown on the hard concrete floor. Zephyr turned her over, brushing the dirt off her mouth and cheeks. She circled her sister's wrist with her fingers, checking her pulse. Zelda's heartbeat was strong. Zephyr scooted over on her bottom, placing her sister's head in her lap. Her hands were shaking. She was afraid what they might do to her and Zelda. They were virgins.

Zelda stirred, mumbled something then sat bolt upright. She was disoriented and frightened. Zelda struggled to get up.

Zephyr clutched her arm, placing a hand over her sister's mouth. "Be still. Keep your voice down."

"Where are we?"

"I don't know. We've been kidnapped."

"I'm afraid."

Zelda was trembling. Zephyr pulled Zelda against her breasts, brushing her sister's hair with her fingers, comforting the terrified young woman.

"I'm afraid too, but we have to keep our heads. I'm sure all they want is money."

"Do you think … Do you think they'll …"

"I don't think so. I hope not."

"I'm so scared. I think I'm going to be sick to my stomach."

"Now stop that. You have to be strong. We both have to be strong if we're going to get through this."

"You're the strong one, Zephyr. I was never like you."

"We're twins, remember? What I am, you're made of the same stuff."

"Oh God, I hope they don't … you know."

"Just keep your head, girl. Trust your instincts."

"I trust you, Zephyr. I always have."

"I love you, little sister. We'll make it together."

A door opened. They were blinded by the bright light. A man walked over, grabbed Zelda's wrist and yanked her to her feet. In the dim light he looked Greek or Russian, maybe Middle Eastern. Zelda tried to jerk away, but he was too strong.

"You're coming with me!"

Zephyr sprang to her feet. The man struck her viciously, knocking her down on the concrete. She saw stars, tasting blood in her mouth. He dragged Zelda out the door, kicking and fighting.

Minutes passed. Suddenly she felt a sharp pain low in her belly. She knew what they were doing to her twin sister. She knew!

⤳

Winston was on the telephone with Rico in Miami. "They have my little girls."

"Ruth called an hour ago. We're working on it. She has an FBI investigator that's on his way to Atlanta. Mike Stroud is his name. He'll be there Wednesday. Stroud is one of the best in the business. Give him a place to sleep. Harry's on the way too. He'll get there this afternoon. Cotton will be there tomorrow. Between him and Stroud we'll find your little girls."

"Thank you, my friend! Anything I have, Rico, anything."

"You owe me nothing. We'll get them back, Winston."

Dutch and Trudy were standing beside Winston, fear splotched across their faces. The police had been in and out half a dozen times. Thus far they had nothing to go on, no ransom note demanding money, no clues, just nothing.

Winston led them back to the library. "I suggest we have a brandy."

Winston performed the honors, handing a glass to Trudy then one to Dutch. Trudy began to cry again. Dutch placed an arm around his wife's shoulders, sitting solemnly beside her on the couch.

"Help is on the way, Trudy. An FBI man is coming Wednesday. Rico says he's one of the best. Cottonmouth will be here tomorrow. Cotton and his partner were the finest Miami ever had."

"Oh, Daddy, I'm terrified for them. They're so young and innocent."

Dutch downed his drink in one gulp. "I wish we could do something. I feel so damned helpless."

"I know, son. I feel the same way. But we're fortunate to have Rico's men helping us. And we have a good detective on the way. Ruth told me about Stroud once before. He's a former Marine and tough as nails.

John Franklin scares the daylights out of people. Those two will get our babies back."

There was a knock at the front door. Dutch went to open it. Harry Vento was standing there with a suitcase in his hand.

$\backsim$

Fat Mike in Miami had been on the telephone for two days. He'd called his connections across the South, asking about sexual predators, inquiring about recent kidnappings. Winston Peters had enemies. Those avenues were investigated.

Mike Stroud was downtown in the FBI office, searching back three years through the records. Reading boring Bureau reports proved a waste of time, so he drove out to the high school. From the school he started backtracking in the direction of Winston Peter's home. A half mile from the parking lot he noticed something partially covered with leaves down a red clay embankment. It was Zelda's school satchel. He started door to door.

Stroud spent the rest of the day waiting for homeowners to come home from work. An elderly woman down the street said she saw a white van parked on the side of the road the day of the disappearance. She didn't know about a driver, but she did say it had a Hertz emblem on the side of the vehicle.

An hour later Stroud had the name of a suspect, A'zam Hussein Baz. He didn't bother with the Atlanta FBI. Mike called Ruth at Langley, who telephoned Rico in Miami. Ruth gave Rico Mike Stroud's private cell phone number.

"Michael Stroud?"

"Yeah, who's this?"

"My name's Enrico Basilio. I'm Ruth Townsend's friend."

"You the Miami dude?"

"That is correct."

"What can I do for ya, Rico?"

"I know Baz. We had a run-in back in the eighties."

"Jesus Christ! This is my lucky day."

"Listen, I'll fly in Saturday. Baz is a Muslim from Saudi Arabia. I'll bring you his information."

"I'll pick you up at the airport. What flight are you on?"

"Delta flight 77, 1:15, Saturday afternoon."

Mike said so long then headed for Winston's home on West Paces Ferry.

⤸

Harry Vento opened the front door. Cottonmouth stood in the foyer behind Harry. Harry was wearing a shoulder holster with his .455 British Webley.

"Damn, you people look like gangsters."

"Come on in, Mike. You find out anything?"

"Your boss knows the bastard."

"Who is 'e?"

"His name is Baz. Rico said he's from Saudi Arabia."

"I'll be damned! Dat's da raghead shit we turned loose to go back an' tell his pals we'd bury their dead asses wid pig guts if they ever come back to America."

"Pig guts?"

"Muslims can't get in Paradise wid dirty souls. Pig guts do da job."

"Mister Peters bought uh honey baked ham, potato salad, collard greens, okra, sliced tomatoes."

"Got any beer?"

"We got a fridge full."

"Rico told me he'd be here tomorrow."

"We know. Him and Mister Peters been talkin'."

They went out in the kitchen and Stroud fixed himself a plate. Cotton pulled out three Blue Ribbons, and they sat down at the kitchen table.

"What do you know about this Baz character?"

"Dis started back when a bunch uh dem Muslims come to Miami to knock off Cottonmouth an' McCoy. Dey was detectives back den, bustin' drug shipments an' shit.

"Eddie Nails, one uh our boys, helped us toast da first batch. Den another herd showed up. Winston come up wid dis pig number. Rico checked it out, an' it sounded real good. Black Jack Pershing was supposed to uh put down uh rebellion in da Philippines buryin' dead ragheads wid pig guts.

"Anyway, we nailed 'em out on Dixie Highway. McCoy got killed an' two uh Rico's boys. Den we cut Baz loose so he could go back an' tell his pig story. Dis time I'm gonna bury his ass fer sure wid Miss Piggy!"

"Ever hear of the Council on American-Islamic Relations?"

"No."

"It's a Muslim terrorist front based in Washington, DC. Our politicians been kissin' their hairy asses for years. They're too damn dumb to investigate who funds the sorry bastards. Ruth Townsend and George Brown got their number three or four years ago."

"You think Baz is connected?"

"It wouldn't surprise me none. They're all a gang uh butchers."

"When da boss gets here we'll nail dat dirtbag. I got a place all picked out for 'im down in Bayou Land."

⌒

Zelda had stopped crying. She'd been raped by two young men. They hurt her. They slapped her around, calling her "infidel," telling her she must "accept the Prophet." Promising they would come back tomorrow for "more schooling."

"It hurt so bad I thought I'd die. They were horrible. They're like animals!"

"Try and relax a little. I wish I could do more to make you comfortable."

"I shouldn't say this, but I'm glad you're with me. I couldn't stand it without you, Zephyr."

"I know, baby. I wish we had Gran-paw's shotgun."

"He said they're coming back in the morning."

"Try not to think about it. Close your eyes and dream about home, about Gran-paw and Mama and Daddy. Think about your cheerleading."

Zephyr was sitting with her back against the wall. Zelda was lying on the floor with her head in Zephyr's lap. She was gently massaging Zelda's temples and brushing her hair with her fingertips. In the half-light their eyes became adjusted to their surroundings. They were in a basement. In the far corner sat a furnace. Nearby was a stack of wood for the fireplace upstairs.

Night fell and Zelda drifted off to sleep. Zephyr could hear the crickets chirping outside. The tiny creatures reminded her of a camping trip they'd been on with the Girl Scouts. It was chilly in the dark basement. The furnace came on, and the basement warmed up some. Zephyr nodded off in a dream.

She dreamed about the night Mister Cottonmouth came to their bedroom. He was huge and scary-looking, but he was so nice they liked him anyway. He said he was there to protect them against the bad people. Zelda went up and sat on his knee. Zephyr climbed up on his other knee. He hugged them, asking how old they were. Four, they told him. They talked a little then he tucked them both into bed.

Sometime in the morning the bad man broke out their window and climbed inside. Mister Cottonmouth grabbed the bad man, knocking him down on the floor and kicking him really hard. Then Mister Cottonmouth threw him back out the window. She and Zelda were frightened and started crying. He did something then she would always remember. He picked them up and kissed them. Then he placed them back under the covers.

Zephyr jerked awake when the door opened. The same man appeared. He walked over, grabbed Zelda by the arm, and pulled her toward the door. Zelda began fighting, kicking and punching her tormentor. Zephyr jumped up, striking the man on the back of his head with her shoe. She kicked his leg, hard. The man swung around, smashing his fist into her face.

When Zephyr came to, the lights were still on. During the melee the man had neglected to turn them off. She began experiencing a familiar ache in her lower belly. They were raping her sister again. She got to her feet. Her left eye was swollen partially shut. Exploring the perimeter of their basement prison she discovered a rusty toolbox sitting behind the gas furnace.

⸺

"Hi ya, boss."

"Hello there, Harry … Cotton."

Harry led the way into the library.

Winston greeted his old friend, bringing him and Mike up to date on the police investigation. It was going nowhere. Then he asked Rico to explain to Michael what he knew about Middle Eastern culture. Cottonmouth brought out four cold ones, and everyone took a seat.

"This is what we're dealing with, Mike.

"A'zam Hussein Baz is a Wahhabi. Wahhabism is the fundamental religion of Saudi Arabia. They believe in a strict interpretation of the Quran. The Quran is their Bible.

"Sharia law is their legal code. No deviation from the Quran is tolerated. They practice honor killing. People are stoned to death. They whip people, crucify them. Cut off heads. A person can lose a hand for stealing a loaf of bread. Women who've been raped cannot testify in a Muslim court. Little girls have their clitorises cut out by some of those fanatics."

"You're not serious."

"I'm dead serious. Islam is a twisted religious order. Women are used for sex and bearing children. They're forbidden from leaving the house unescorted. Women are owned by their husbands, like cattle or a dog. They're not allowed to drive a car or go to school. It's a totally male-dominated world.

"Those people are as backward today as they were 1,500 years ago. The majority are ignorant. Religious fanaticism is rampant. Inbreeding is everywhere. Islam is not a religion of peace like we've been led to believe. The Quran, if taken literally, is a recipe for slavery and war."

Mike exploded. "What a crock uh shit!"

"Baz was a fanatic when we turned him loose," Rico said. "God knows what he's become by now.

Mike Stroud and John Franklin drove out to the Hertz rental office in Norcross. They had photos of Baz they'd gotten from Interpol. Mike went inside to question the employees. John Franklin went down Peachtree Street asking if anyone had seen the man in the photograph. The Hertz people proved a dead end, so Mike ventured down Buford Highway, asking questions. They spent the rest of the afternoon nosing around Norcross, but that, too, was a dead end. Calling it a day, they stopped at a café on Peachtree Industrial Boulevard for dinner. They were comparing notes when the waitress spoke up, pointing at the picture.

"I know that man."

Mike stood up and handed the lady a twenty dollar bill. She didn't know where Baz lived, but she did offer to get his license number when he returned. Mike promised her a hundred bucks when she delivered. Miss Betty informed them he'd eaten there six or seven times around 6:30 at night.

"We gotta stake out this place," Mike insisted.

"He'll recognize me," John said. "I knocked 'is ass around some."

"I'll do it. It's 8:30 now. I'll come back tomorrow afternoon."

"I'll get us a shotgun, just in case."

"This has given me an appetite. Let's order a steak!"

⌒

At 5:25 the following afternoon Mike was sitting dead in the water on Interstate 285, the Atlanta Perimeter. Driving east from Roswell Road toward Interstate 85, the automobiles were averaging 10 mph. Unaccustomed to the afternoon traffic, he made it to the café parking lot at 6:16 p.m. Inside he met with the waitress, Miss Betty.

"He came early. You just missed him."

"Well, damn!"

"But I got somethin' for ya, honey."

"What?"

"His license number."

Mike grabbed her off the floor and swung Miss Betty around in a circle. The 65-year-old black lady squealed with laughter, hanging on to Michael Stroud for dear life.

"White boy, you be a crazy man."

Mike peeled off five twenties, kissed Miss Betty on the cheek, and ran out the door. Back at Winston's place Mike called the FBI night manager to get the man in charge of auto registration away from his dinner table and back downtown to his Atlanta office. A red 1989 Ford Mustang had been purchased in Suwanee, Georgia, which was about 10 miles NE of Norcross. The owner's signature was Baz. No home address had been given.

"That bastard is somewhere up in those hills."

"Yeah, but where? There are hundreds uh farms an' houses in them hills," Cottonmouth said.

"It's a red Mustang. We got that to go on."

"If we split up an' drive separate cars we'll cover twice as much ground." Cottonmouth posed another question. "What about Winston an' Dutch Henry?"

"They're too involved. You an' me and a few agents from downtown can canvass the whole area in two or three days. We can use the helicopter some, but I don't want to tip our hand."

"That sounds good. Winston's too old, an' Dutch might blunder in an' get the girls killed. Flyovers ever' three or four hours oughta do tha job. He'll think it's them bank helicopters."

At 6:30 the next morning Mike, John, and four FBI agents set out in six nondescript automobiles for Suwanee, Georgia.

⌒

Zelda lay on her side, physically exhausted. Both men had raped her again. It hurt to move her legs.

"They kept ranting and raving, 'accept the Prophet.' Then they beat me some more, calling me 'the infidel whore.'"

They were finally given bread and water after having nothing to eat or drink for two days. Zephyr was dipping pieces of bread in the water bowl, feeding them to her sister. The bread was hard and stale, but the water made it palatable.

"I can't … It hurts too much … They're killing me."

Tears ran down Zephyr's cheeks. She was beginning to fear that was the purpose the horrible men had in store for her and Zelda. But why, she wondered. Why were they being so cruel?

⌒

She and Zelda knew nothing about Rico and his men, Cottonmouth and McCoy, or Winston and John Parker. They had killed all nine of the assassin squad A'zam Baz had flown into Miami with to murder Franklin and McCoy. Baz had been captured. He went to pieces during threats of being shot and buried with pig entrails. He believed his unclean soul would never be allowed to enter Paradise if his remains were buried with pig guts. He cried, begging them to spare him. Rico planned it that way, sending him back to Saudi Arabia with his pig story. Resentment and shame had grown over the years. During that time he'd risen in the ranks of the Wahhabis. A'zam Hussein Baz was now a mullah, preaching the word of the Quran.

The best way to gain revenge on his captors, he reasoned, was to torture and kill their loved ones. He has chosen Winston Peters after assigning Muslim spies to investigate the gunfight on Dixie Highway. He was going to try for Rico's children next, and after that John Parker's daughter.

⌒

Zelda had discovered a small screw driver in the toolbox. It was a flat head with a three-inch shank. She ground the head back and forth against the concrete floor. The handle measured two and a half inches.

The next morning he came again for Zelda. This time Zephyr was beaten unconscious by both guards. When Zelda was dragged back and thrown down on the concrete, she was in shock. Zephyr lay beside her sister through the night holding her close, sharing her body warmth with Zelda. When sunlight flooded through the window, Zelda was conscious but in terrible pain. She was bleeding. They had torn something inside her.

Then the door opened, and the man appeared.

"She's had it," Zephyr told him. "She's no good anymore. I never liked the bitch anyway. Take me. I want to experience sex with two handsome men."

Zephyr pulled up her skirt, revealing her feminine beauty. She was wearing no panties.

Down the hall they went to a room with a twin bed, four chairs, and a table laden with wine bottles. She lay down on the mattress, spreading her legs apart.

The guard placed his revolver on the table, and pulled off his pants and underwear. The second guard shoved a chair over beside the door and leaned back against the wall.

"Come on, big boy. I want you to fuck me."

He mounted Zephyr. It Hurt!

He was rough and clumsy, but eager for the sex. She clamped her eyes shut, gritting her teeth, placing her left forearm behind his neck. His sexual thrusts burned inside her like bee stings.

With all her might, she drove the screwdriver into the man's neck, right up to its wooden handle. She yanked it out and thrust again, and again. He squalled like a stricken animal! The guard fell backward off his chair. Zephyr shoved her rapist to the floor. Blood was spurting from his throat.

The guard stumbled to his feet, fumbling for his pistol. Zephyr had the revolver in her hand, squeezing the trigger. Her first shot hit the door. The second bullet struck the chair. Her third round tore away part of his face. He screamed and fell. Zephyr ran and stood over the man, firing a fatal shot into his head. Then she turned and shot the bleeding man on the floor, twice. The revolver clicked empty.

Chapter Eleven

Zephyr

Major General Robert Kurtz and Lieutenant General Jack Marshal were seated in a rear booth in the avant-garde watering hole on D Street known as The Jug. The men wore jeans and sport coats so as not to be recognized as military. On the wall above them hung a poster of Jimi Hendrix setting his guitar on fire at the Monterey Pop Festival. Beside Jimi was an aging photograph of Big Brother and the Holding Company with Janis Joplin. Pink Floyd's "Comfortably Numb" was playing on the Wurlitzer out front. The place was nearly empty. The crowd didn't come in until around 5:30.

Marshal asked, "What's your take on the situation?"

"Half-assed," Kurtz replied. "Reagan peaked in '85 with *Star Wars*. That put Ivan out of business. Bush cut defense spending four years in a row. Now we've got Clinton who's certainly no friend of the military. He's cut the Army by eight divisions, Air Force Wings from 24 to 13, and our ships are down from 600 to less than 300. We still have the best armed forces in the world, but our planners need to concentrate on developing the smart stuff as opposed to a wide range of platforms like we had in the '50s and '60s.

"I agree. I don't like those 9mm side arms either. We need the old .45 back."

"Yes, and we need to upgrade the M-16. McNamara screwed that up like everything else him and his Whiz Kids touched. He and Johnson were two peas in a pod, lying to the Joint Chiefs, lying to the public, lying to Congress while running the war straight into the ground. LBJ was an insecure man preoccupied with his domestic programs. McNamara was both arrogant and ignorant. He didn't understand Ho Chi Minh, China, or Vietnam. They should have listened to Curtis LeMay and General Greene and blown Hanoi and Haiphong off the map, or pulled up stakes and got the hell out."

"*Dereliction of Duty*. You told me to read it, remember?" Marshal reminded Kurtz

"Right, I'd forgotten that."

"At least we have the F-22 coming on-line. That's going to be a game changer."

"What about Uriah Frank? You heard from him lately?" Bob Kurtz asked.

"Uriah and Lydia Sams are working together in London. They got their hands full with all those nut jobs pouring in from the East. That's gonna develop into a real shit storm."

"It already has. People don't see what's right under their nose."

"Bob, if our politicians don't wake up we're going to be in World War III in ten or twelve years. Islam tried it twice before. Now they're at it again."

"I don't see the politicians changing a thing. Political correctness is just another excuse for doing nothing. Don't rock the boat. Vote for me. Bullshit!"

"I studied Hitler and Mussolini. Churchill sounded the alarm all through the 1930s. All Parliament did was sit on their fat asses and drink tea. If Hitler had promoted his 262 jet fighter and his Tiger tank, they'd have kicked our asses clear to Sunday."

"At least Muslims don't have those capabilities, just oil."

"Yeah, but what do you do with over a billion assholes?"

"That's above my pay grade, Jack."

"What do you think about that dirtbag in Laredo?"

"I think we should contact Ruth Townsend. Carlos may be a security threat."

"I'll call Ruth and have her look into it."

"Drink up. There's an Irish pub two blocks over."

Zephyr crept up to the first floor. The coast was clear. She began searching the house. Zelda needed medical attention and something to eat. She found Tylenol, a bottle of red wine, and snack food in the kitchen. Then she noticed the cottage out back with its lights on. She stood behind the curtains and watched. A man appeared through a window. She gathered her supplies and hurried back down the stairs.

A'zam Baz took great pleasure in studying his Quran while the soldiers who accompanied him from Saudi Arabia carried out his instructions next door. They were to rape the women and starve them, but only if they weren't menstruating. The Quran forbade the rape of captive females during their menstrual cycles. Then he was going to hang them and leave them for Winston Peters to identify.

Shakespeare had written, "Revenge is a dish best served cold." A'zam Baz was going to serve Winston Peters with his granddaughters, cold and brutally murdered.

"You have to walk. We've got to get out of here. I saw one next door."

"I can't … It hurts too much …"

"Zelda, I won't leave you. Now get up!"

Zephyr helped her sister to her feet. Blood started down her right leg.

Zelda took a few steps. "God, it hurts."

"I know, baby. Hold on to me."

In the hall Zephyr led her toward a door at the end of the hallway. She sat Zelda on a chair then ran upstairs. She remembered seeing candles in the living room on a round wooden table, with matches and plates of partially eaten food. She lit two of the candles then ran down the stairs to their basement prison. With a stick of kindling she knocked loose the gas connection from the furnace. It made a hissing sound.

"Come on, baby, hold tight."

They stumbled out the door and into the woods. Night was beginning to fall. The temperature was 58 degrees.

⌒

Mike was on his cell phone to Cotton. "Any sign of that Mustang?"

"I've seen ever' thing but a damn Mustang."

"Keep at it, we'll find it."

⌒

Zelda was having a terrible time walking on the uneven terrain. Each time she stumbled she whimpered with pain. Zephyr was supporting her as best she could, but blood had run down into Zelda's shoe, making their progress even more difficult. Her loafer kept sliding off. Seventy yards from the house they paused to rest. Zephyr cleaned her sister's bloody shoe with moss she gathered from an outcrop of rock. A quarter mile in the distance they could see lights. The women were both exhausted.

When the house exploded Baz was knocked off his chair. He leapt up, looking out to see yellow flames leaping high into the night sky.

"Infidel Whores! They've done this!"

He snatched up a .22 rifle and burst out the door. At the far end of the burning building he searched among the leaves and pine needles. There! He saw blood. It was them. He ran deeper among the trees then stopped and listened. Nothing! He continued another twenty paces. Nothing!

⌐

"We've got to go on. There's a house down there."

"I can't. I can't do it."

"No! You're coming with me."

Zephyr pulled her sister to her feet. Zelda sagged against her. Then fell. Zephyr pulled her up again, hoisting her up piggyback. Zephyr set off with her 118-pound burden toward the lights. Thirty yards behind them A'zam Baz thought he heard something.

⌐

"Cotton? You see that?"

"I sure as hell do. That's got to be them."

They were looking at a red glow on the horizon. The back roads they were driving on converged at an intersection. Cotton ditched his Mercury and got in with Mike. They sped on toward the fire.

⌐

"You can't make it with me. I'm too heavy."

"You're not heavy. You're my little sister."

"I hear something."

Zephyr paused. She heard it too. He was close.

"We've got to hide."

Frantically she hurried on with Zelda clinging to her shoulders. Zephyr stumbled and fell.

"Quick! Under there."

They crawled under a clutch of camellia plants.

Baz strode into the clearing. He knew they were there. He poked his rifle several times in a cluster of magnolia bushes. Then he punched a broad clump of kudzu. When he jabbed the camellias, something soft gave way beneath his gun barrel.

"Come out, bitch. I know you're there." He reached in, dragging Zelda out by her foot. She cried out in pain.

Zephyr crawled out and sat beside Zelda, her arms around her sister. He eyed them with hatred. With his captives shivering at his feet, A'zam Hussein Baz began reciting the Quran.

"'O people of the Book, do not be fanatical in your faith, and say nothing but the truth about Allah. The Messiah who is Jesus, son of Mariam, was only a messenger of Allah, nothing more. He bestowed His Word on Mariam and His Spirit. So believe in Allah and say not Trinity, for Allah is one God.

"'The punishment for those who wage war against Allah and His Prophet and reject Islam, is to murder them, crucify them, or cut off a hand and a foot on opposite sides … their doom is dreadful. They will not escape the fire, suffering constantly.

"'They are surely infidels who say, 'God is the Christ, the Messiah, the son of Mary.'

"'Fight and slay the Pagans, seize them, beleaguer them, and lie in wait for them in every stratagem. For them garments of fire shall be cut and there shall be poured over their heads boiling water whereby whatever is in the bowels and skin shall be dissolved and they will be punished with hooked iron rods.

"'Surely the vilest of animals in Allah's sight are those who disbelieve.

"'Murder them and treat them harshly.

"'Allah is the only God.'"

A'zam drew a hunting knife from a leather sheath attached to his belt. The blade was silvery and glistened in the moonlight

"Your time has come, Whores of Babylon. Your presence on earth is an abomination against Allah."

He reached for Zephyr's hair …

Blam!

His knife hand exploded in a cloud of flesh, bone, and blood.

Baz let out a high-pitched scream.

"I bet that smarts some, don't it?"

Cottonmouth stepped out of the bushes with a 12-gauge in his hand. Mike Stroud was right behind him with his .45. Zelda struggled to her feet, grabbing onto Cottonmouth, tears flooding down her cheeks. Zephyr flung her arms around Mike's neck, sobbing like a little baby. She had held it together for Zelda and herself as long as she could.

Seven days passed before Zelda was released from Piedmont Hospital. Zephyr had spent three days in the same room with Zelda before she was declared well enough to leave. Winston had arranged for Mike and Cotton to be there when Dutch and Trudy brought Zelda home. Michael and Cottonmouth were standing in the living room when Winston escorted her in.

Not saying a word, Zelda walked across the room, placing her arms around Cotton, and stood there, holding him, with her eyes closed.

Finally, she spoke. "Twice you've saved me and my sister. There are no words. 'Thank you' is not enough. We will always be in your debt, Mister Cottonmouth, always. And you and Michael will always be in our prayers."

For the first time since his partner was killed, John Franklin got misty-eyed. "If I had me uh daughter, I'd want her to be just like you,

Zelda. An' you too, Zephyr. I reckon, in a way, you are my daughters. Leastways, it feels like it."

"Yes, we are, Mister Cottonmouth, and we always will be," Zephyr said. She hugged Cotton. Then Michael.

Cottonmouth had carried Zelda out of the woods to the automobile. Mike had helped Zephyr to the car then went back for Baz. A'zam was bandaged and locked in the trunk.

"This is the happiest day of my life," Trudy said. "Thank God you're finally home."

Dutch stepped forward to shake their hands yet again. "Fellas, you're welcome to stay here with us anytime you're in Atlanta."

Then Winston made an offer nobody could refuse. "I think the girls, I should say ladies, are old enough now for a glass of my good brandy."

⌒

A'zam Baz was sitting on a mound of black dirt in front of an open grave. He was too weak to stand. The stump of his forearm was heavily bandaged where his right hand used to be. He had been treated in Atlanta by Dr. Margot Bach, flown in from Miami, then shot full of morphine for a trip to Slidell. Harry Vento drove the Ford Bronco. Moses Blue Pony and Karl Musgrove had dug the grave before Harry got there. The grave was situated on a secluded island far out in the Louisiana bayou.

"Got any last words?"

"You can't do this. I'm a mullah. I preach the Holy Word."

"You'll be preachin' uh different tune 'fore long."

"You're a nonbeliever. You blaspheme against Islam."

"Fuck Islam!"

"I'm Muhammad's messenger. Infidels must accept the Prophet."

"Yer stinkin' religion ain't worth dog vomit."

"Allah is the only god."

"Well, fuck him too!"

"Blasphemer! You insult the Holy One!"

Blue Pony walked up with a five-gallon bucket he had hidden behind a stand of cattails.

"I have rights … What's that?"

"Pig guts. You ain't gettin' no virgins, pally."

A'zam Hussein Baz went crazy, screaming and shouting for Allah to save him. A vision of hell descended. Paradise and A'zam's bandwagon of 72 virgins was about to fly the coop.

Harry leveled his .455 Webley and squeezed the trigger. Baz tumbled backward into the hole. Blue Pony dumped in the contents of the bucket—then threw in the bucket. Karl handed out shovels, and they set about filling the grave.

Chapter Twelve

Bobbi

Most nights Zelda would awaken drenched with sweat, crying and disoriented. The nightmares persisted. Dutch and Winston decided to move Zephyr's bed into Zelda's bedroom. That first night Zelda awoke soaking wet, crying out for her mother. Zephyr took off her wet pajamas and put her into clean ones. Zephyr got into bed with Zelda and held her until she drifted to sleep. This continued for two weeks.

"I'm sorry I'm such a burden."

"You're not a burden. You're my little sister."

"I keep dreaming about those terrible men."

"I know."

"I thought I was going to die, and you saved me."

"It was pretty awful in those woods. Then Mister Cottonmouth and Michael saved us both."

"Do you think a nice man will ever want me for his wife?"

"You were raped, Zelda. There's a big difference."

"But still, I feel kinda, you know … dirty."

"I haven't told anybody, but one of them was screwing me before I stabbed him and got his gun. I shot both those guards. And I don't feel one bit dirty!"

"Goodness gracious, Zephyr. I didn't know."

"If I can live with killing two men, you can live with the other."

"I'm glad you told me. I don't feel so … so alone anymore."

"You were never alone. I would have died for you."

Zelda started crying. Zephyr wept too, holding her sister in her arms, sitting cross-legged together on the bed.

"Do you mind sleeping with me again tonight?"

Zephyr snuggled under the covers, again placing her arms around her twin. "It was awful, wasn't it?"

"Oh my yes, but you were so strong. You were wonderful."

"We're made of the same stuff, little sister. What you went through was much worse. But you came through it like a champion. That makes you very special."

"I feel lucky to be your twin. I love you so much."

"Someday we'll both have families, and we'll look back on this like a bad dream."

"I hope so. I want a little boy and a little girl."

"That's the spirit. And you'll have a wonderful husband."

"I want us both to have wonderful husbands and live in Buckhead and have wonderful children."

"Keep thinking that way, girl. We'll have it someday."

"Good night, Zephyr."

"Good night, little sister."

The twins snuggled together and slept.

⌒

Zelda's menstrual periods had started five months before she and her twin were kidnapped. Her cycles commenced around the twenty-first of every month. Since coming home from the hospital, no periods had appeared. This had just dawned on Zelda.

Immediately she went to consult Zephyr. "I might be pregnant."

"Think! When was your last period?"

"Two months ago, maybe longer."

"You've got to be tested. I'll go with you."

"Shouldn't we tell Mom and Dad first?"

"Not yet, but we have to tell Gran-paw. He'll know what to do."

Winston Peters showed concern when told, but he was quaking inside with emotions. He made a telephone call. Then the three of them drove over to the Emory Clinic on Clifton Road in Midtown. Doctor Johnson received them in his office above the parking lot.

"Zelda, you're in your first trimester, five to seven weeks along. Your health is excellent, and everything looks normal. You're going to have a fine baby."

Zelda sat down on a chair. Zephyr placed a hand on her sister's shoulder. Winston took Doctor Johnson to another room and explained the situation. Abortion was discussed, adoption, and the possibility of keeping the child. When they returned, Zephyr and Zelda were involved in an animated conversation. The men stepped back, closing the door, allowing the young ladies their privacy. Several minutes elapsed. Zephyr opened the door, asking the men to come inside.

"Gran-paw, you always taught us about doing the right thing. This little person in my tummy is innocent of what happened to me and Zephyr. We both want the baby."

Winston turned and looked at Johnson. Doctor Johnson nodded his head, smiling.

Gran-paw puddled up. "Don't this beat all? My grandbabies are all grown up."

Then the twins shed tears. The girls hugged Gran-paw. Then they hugged Doctor Johnson.

Doctor Johnson laughed. "I must say, this is one exceptional pair of young ladies. I'd be honored to be your doctor, Zelda."

"Yes, doctor, I want you to help me along with my little one."

"I wish more women were like you, Zelda. You're quite the rare commodity in today's world."

Zephyr was confused. "Am I gonna be a godmother or a godaunt? What am I?"

Zelda teased her. "You're my fairy god sister."

Zelda had found a new purpose in life. Their time in the basement had forged a bond between the twins not unlike what soldiers experience in combat. The months ahead would provide moments of wonder and great joy. Through the fire two strong individuals had emerged. Dutch and Trudy were in for a grand adventure.

∽

Uriah was seated at a table at The Old Bell on Fleet Street having lunch with Lydia Sams. MI-6 had assigned Lydia the task of investigating the growing influx of Africans and Middle Easterners. There was growing concern at 10 Downing Street regarding the nation's resources, and a growing Muslim community demanding Sharia law. She recorded the numbers and nationalities with assistance from obliging intelligence agencies. Those included Germany, France, Spain, and Morocco. Uriah Frank was on loan from Mossad to assist Lydia Sams with her duties. Neither England nor Israel had any notion about their roles as assassins with the group in America.

"That son of a bitch funds 175 different organizations, everything from the Tides Foundation to Amnesty International. George Soros and those Rothschilds are a menace to the entire world!" Lydia declared.

"Lydia, they're just one more facet of the Evil Empire."

"I've had it with those douche bags."

"The group knows who they are. There's too much of a risk involved."

"What is the one thing they covet, besides power?"

"You mean money?"

"Greed is their Achilles heel. If we can find a way to tap into their money supply, they'll be jumping out windows like it was Black Tuesday."

Uriah thought for several moments. "Bobbi!"

"Who?"

"Bobbi works with Mossad."

"What are you jabbering about?"

"Bobbi is the code name for Abe Lieberman. He's a computer wizard. If anyone can break into one of their banking systems, Bobbi can."

"How might we go about that?"

"I'd have to take it before my superiors."

"What would you tell them?"

"We'd have to reveal what we know about Soros, the Rothschilds, and the Bilderbergs."

Lydia was skeptical. "And how would you explain knowing that?"

"I'm not sure. We'd have to get permission from Ruth Townsend."

"I could say we worked together and shared information."

"Mossad would ask for proof."

"This is getting too complicated, Uriah."

"Ruth would have to cover her end. I don't like all this exposure."

"Neither do I. Could you go to Bobbi direct?"

"I hadn't thought of that. It's worth a try."

"It would expose us somewhat."

"Bobbi's a genius. He keeps secrets. He has to or some husband might shoot him."

"He sounds like a bloody horn toad."

"That he is, and tripping up Mister Soros might just appeal to Mister Horn Toad."

"Where could we hide the money?"

"Let's approach Bobbi first, and see if he's interested."

⌣

Five months into her pregnancy Zelda had a bump on her tummy. At least that's what Zephyr called it. Doctor Johnson had determined the infant was a boy. Zephyr was as excited over the coming event as if it were her own baby. In a way it was since both twins had been raped by the same guard.

"Sometimes it feels like butterflies."

"Does your stomach move?"

"No, it's all inside. It's hard to explain."

"Next time it happens, I want to feel it."

"Okay, if you're in another part of the house, I'll yell."

"The school will freak when they find out you're pregnant."

"I know. I can't do my cheerleading much longer."

"Maybe if we said you were sick, and you dropped out the rest of the year."

"Let's ask Gran-paw. Daddy would just get embarrassed again. He's so funny."

"You can't blame him or Mom. You're still their little girl."

"It's hard for them, I know that. It was awful when Gran-paw told Mom and she cried."

"Don't worry, Zelda. When the little boy comes, they'll both love him."

"He's doing it again … Feel … feel me!" Zelda pulled up her top.

Zephyr placed both hands on Zelda's stomach. "I think I feel something. Yes … it is like a butterfly."

⌣

Gran-paw was in his library when the twins walked in, seeking advice. Winston had been weighing the decision of telling Dutch about the group. High blood pressure had appeared over the past year, which Winston kept to himself. If he died, the group would lose a valuable player as well as their Atlanta base.

"Gran-paw, I'm starting to show a little. Zephyr suggested I drop out of school and pretend I'm sick. Do you think I should let the school know I'm pregnant?"

"Honey, that's the $64,000 question."

"If we told we were kidnapped an' stuff, would it make us look bad?" Zephyr asked.

"Reputations are funny things. Once damaged, they're hard to make right again."

"So you don't think I should tell?"

"Zelda, I believe you should do what your heart tells you to do."

"Do you think Mom and Dad will be upset?"

"Some, but if you decide to tell your school chums, I'll handle Mama and Daddy."

"I think we should think about it some more," Zelda declared.

"Good suggestion. You girls talk it over then come tell me what you decide."

The twins retired to Zelda's bedroom. The nightmares had almost gone away, but Zephyr still slept with her sister. She was always there those nights Zelda did awaken, afraid and crying in their basement prison. Winston's therapist had helped Zelda confront the horrors of being raped and nearly murdered. Still, the nightmares came and went. Zephyr harbored no regrets over killing the two guards.

"Should we tell?"

"I don't know. What do you think?"

"I don't think our friends will be ashamed of us, Zephyr. I believe most of the school would understand."

"Some won't, but who cares about them."

"It's like Gran-paw says. Some people like you and some don't no matter what you do."

"You'll be the center of attention, that's for sure. Me too, I guess."

"Zephyr, you saved my life. What do you want to do?"

"I'm with you, Zelda. Whatever you want."

"I think we should."

"Then we will. No more hiding in the shadows."

"Are you sure?"

"I believe it's the right thing to do. We've done nothing wrong. And we're bringing a little guy into the world. You make me proud, girl."

"Let's go tell Gran-paw."

⌒

Bobbi lit up like a Christmas tree when Lydia walked into the room. "What a rare vision of beauty. Are you spoken for, dear lady?"

Uriah and Lydia had carefully planned their little charade.

"Oh yes, thank you, sir. This is my fiancé, Uriah Frank."

Uriah stepped forward, shaking Bobbi's hand.

"You are quite the fortunate one, young fellow. I envy you."

"Thank you, sir. We have a special favor to ask."

"Then tell old Bobbi what it is you desire."

Half an hour later Abe Lieberman sat pondering the two individuals seated before him. Never in his career had anyone proposed such an outlandish operation. It was fraught with peril, even to the point of getting killed. Yet it presented a magnificent challenge, one to his liking. But was it worth the risk?

"You're both quite insane. You know that, don't you?"

Lydia grinned. "We've been called worse."

"I can understand why. In a caper like this we could all end up with a tag on our big toes."

"What are our lives worth compared to saving the world from those vermin?"

"Woman, you have balls the size of grapefruits!"

Lydia laughed. "Now I've never been told *that* before."

"Well, you do. And so do you, Uriah. If I were younger I'd love to go with you on your adventures. There is one thing, though. The Knesset must never know about my involvement, nor the Mossad. We're each expendable, in one form or fashion. You both know that. We all work with dangerous people."

"Then you'll do it?"

"I would like nothing better than to take that Soros *shmendrik* down a peg or two. But the Rothschilds, there I must proceed with caution. James de Rothschild financed the main Knesset building in his will, which was completed in 1966. I bet you didn't know that, did you?"

"No, sir, we didn't."

"No matter, some of them are as corrupt as the Nazis."

"What about the Bilderbergs?"

"Them too. Some good, some just awful. There are rotten people in both organizations."

"How will you go about it?"

"Leave that to me. I have my ways. They will never know it came from Israel. It will appear, rather obviously, to have come from China or Russia. I'll make that decision later, depending on who's the greater threat at the time."

"How can we thank you, Bobbi?"

"Keep at it, what you do. And stay alive. We need brave *mentshen* like you two."

Lydia kissed his cheek, Bobbi patted her fanny, and they left.

⌒

Gran-paw was pleased with the twins' decision. Their kidnapping had matured them beyond their years. In ways that was good, but it robbed them of any remaining childhood they might have enjoyed. Those Arab fanatics deserved what they got. But there were millions more like them. Winston wondered what would become of his family after he was gone. His blood pressure was getting worse. The time had come to tell Dutch Henry about the group.

"That's about it, Dutch. We're a special group dedicated to preserving the Constitution, capitalism, and our religious freedoms. Evil men are trying to take that away from us. Most of the people who come to this house are part of the group. You already know Rico and Cotton, Harry and a few of the others."

"You didn't have to ask, Winston. I'd follow you or Cotton anywhere. But I don't want Trudy to know, not yet anyway. She has her hands full with the twins, and that baby's coming. Zelda's pregnancy took some getting used to, but Trudy's fine with it now. I'm very proud of my girls, what they went through and their decision to keep the child. They're a lot tougher than I gave them credit for."

"Zephyr and Zelda are the same stock you and I and Trudy come from. Victoria was like that, God rest her soul. We're the people, Dutch, the ones that make this country great. It isn't the politicians or the lawyers and judges. It's the American people, truckers and construction workers, doctors, nurses, soldiers. We make it go.

"I'm counting on you, my boy. I want you to take my place."

"I'm honored, sir."

"Keep your job. That will be your cover. There'll be times when you have to leave the country. I'll take care of that with your employer. You're going to acquire some very influential men and women as your new associates."

"You've about blown me away, Winston."

"Son, after what you and Trudy went through with those pirates, I haven't a thing to fret about. There are two men at the Pentagon I want you to get to know. Then there's Ruth Townsend with the Central Intelligence Agency. She just married her partner, George Brown. I'll call Washington in the morning. I want you to fly up there next week."

"You seem in an awful hurry, Winston."

"I am in a hurry, son. Doc Underwood told me I have five or six months to live."

"Jesus! Isn't there something he can do? What about a specialist?"

"It's my heart. The darn thing's worn out."

"Can't you get another heart, a transplant?"

"There's something else. I've been diagnosed with early stage Parkinson's. Victoria had Alzheimer's. I won't put the family through that again."

"I wish there was something I could do."

"There is, my boy. Memorize the things I tell you while there's still time. Harry's wife, Margot, has promised to come give me a shot if I linger. I want you to call her if that happens."

A second promise was given Mister Peters.

Dutch had tears in his eyes. The man he loved and respected was going to die. A great responsibility lay before Dutch Henry, far more of a challenge than anything he'd faced before. Protecting America with such a small force was mind boggling.

⌒

Lydia Sams lived in a two-bedroom flat overlooking the River Thames near Waterloo Bridge. Her quaint living quarters wasn't very far from Trafalgar Square, where she often spent time feeding the pigeons. Most days she worked from her computer. MI-6 had secured her telephone line when the computer was installed. Two months had gone by since her and Uriah's meeting with Bobbi.

A Star of David appeared on her computer screen.

Greetings, Fair Lady
I'm happy to report success. These funds are untraceable. Here
is your account number and your passwords. The bank will ask
no questions. Use this money for the group's war against evildo-
ers. God Speed.

Lydia typed in sixteen numbers and letters followed by two passwords, Blue Skies.

She rose from her chair, staring at the computer screen in disbelief. Then she plopped back down in her seat. Her account balance read $4,494,776,512.00.

Bobbi had siphoned off nearly four and a half billion dollars from someplace, or some places, before the fail-safe systems shut down his hacking. She went straight out to the kitchen and poured herself a glass of gin. Then she called Uriah on his cell phone.

London

Newspapers around the world picked up on the story of a suicide in one of the major banks in the Cayman Islands. A manager had shot himself over the loss of a considerable amount of money. Speculation surfaced that foul play was involved. When Ruth Townsend was informed of the truth by Lydia Sams, Ruth called Winston Peters in Atlanta. Winston summoned Dutch to his library.

"I have around thirteen million in the bank, but this is nothing short of a miracle. Now we have the financial means to carry out plans we once thought impossible. I'll leave it to you and Ruth and Rico to carry on in my behalf. I'm going to die a very happy man."

"You're not allowed to die yet, sir! You have to see the baby when he's born. Zelda and Zephyr need you. Trudy and I need you too."

"I'm proud of you, Dutch. You and my family are going to be just fine."

Dutch hugged his father-in-law, and kissed him on his cheek.

Three weeks later Zelda went into labor. Dutch and Trudy were at Lenox Square picking out baby clothes.

"Gran-paw! It's time! I have to go to the hospital."

"Oh Lord, where're my keys? Zephyr! I need you!"

Zephyr came running down the stairs from her bedroom. "What's wrong?"

"Zelda's having her baby. I can't find my car keys."

Zephyr grabbed them off the kitchen counter and dashed for the garage. "Come on, I've got them."

Winston bundled Zelda into the backseat then jumped in beside her. Zephyr drove. They made it to Piedmont Hospital in four minutes flat, driving around traffic with their signals flashing and running two red lights. Zelda was whisked into Delivery with Zephyr right behind her. Gran-paw commenced pacing the floor in the waiting room.

"It hurts! I need something!"

Zelda was flat of her back with her feet up in the stirrups, her head on a pillow and a concerned expression on her face. A physician had just given Zelda a shot to lessen her pain. Zephyr was the one requesting help for labor pains. Doctor Johnson and the nurses shared a confused look, not knowing what to make of the woman curled up on the delivery room floor.

Zelda explained. "We're twins. We're telepathic. Give her a shot."

Forty-five minutes later the baby arrived, six pounds and seven ounces.

⌒⟶

A blanket of acrid smoke hung above London, remnants of last night's fires. Captain Peters had just pulled into Charing Cross on the subway, which Londoners called the Underground. Plans were to meet with his squadron mates at The Ship & Shovel. Walking from the subway platform to their rendezvous point, he stopped to admire Admiral Nelson's tower in Trafalgar Square. Four bronze lions flanked the tall granite column.

Air raid sirens began their mournful wailing.

He debated whether to continue on or return to Charing Cross. Better go back, he reasoned. Bombs were starting to fall.

Down inside the Underground station he found a place to sit beside a lady and her young daughter. The woman was a widow. Her husband had been killed at Dunkirk. She had a paper bag of fish and chips she offered to share with Winston. He accepted two of her fries.

Two women in WAAC uniforms were standing nearby beside a steel support column. Winston couldn't take his eyes off the shapely blonde.

"Excuse me, my name's Winston Peters. Would you ladies care for a drink after the all clear?"

The WAACs looked at one another, smiled, and nodded their heads.

"Of course, Captain. We'd love to have a drink with you. It's been a dreadful week."

By the time they reached The Ship & Shovel most of his crew had drunk themselves silly. Marsha took a liking to the ball gunner, Sergeant Phelps. The remaining eight crewmen set about searching for companions for the evening. An hour later, Winston whisked Victoria out the pub door and into his life. A flame had been ignited. Love was soon to blossom.

Winston opened his eyes. He'd been dreaming. Zelda was dozing on the library couch with the baby in her arms. Jake was four months old, olive skin, black hair, a beautiful little boy.

Zephyr peeked in the library door. "You're awake, Gran-paw."

"Yes, I was having myself a nice dream."

"Dinner will be ready in few minutes."

"What are we having?"

"Your favorite, fried chicken with mashed potatoes and chicken gravy."

Zelda woke up. "Do you need any help?"

"No! You stay with Jake and Gran-paw."

At the dinner table Winston experienced trouble using his right hand. He knew the symptoms. He'd been having them for more than a week. He finished his fried chicken and mashed potatoes with his left hand. Dutch noticed he was trying to hide it. He followed him into the library where Winston seated himself behind his desk. He asked Dutch to pour them two glasses of brandy.

"Do you want me to call an ambulance?"

"I want you to sit with me and enjoy your drink."

"Sir, I think you need a doctor."

"Do you remember my telling you about that song Vera Lynn sang when Victoria and I went to see her at the Stoll Theatre in London?"

"Yes, but I should call …"

"'We'll Meet Again' was what she sang. Victoria cried. We lost a lot of boys in 1943. I shed a few tears myself. It was a touching and patriotic melody."

"But, Winston …"

"Dutch, I want you to call Margot in Miami and let her know I may need her soon."

"Please, sir, don't do that, not yet."

"You promised."

"I know, but …"

"We'll meet again someday. That's God's plan for the world, son. "

"Let me call Trudy and the girls in, and little Jake."

"All right, if that's what you want."

Dutch composed himself then went out to the kitchen. When he came back with his family, Winston was slumped over sideways in his chair. He'd suffered a heart attack.

Trudy had been informed about her father's request months earlier. It was a terrible thing for her and the twins, but Trudy honored her father's wishes. Harry's wife arrived from Miami the next day. Winston's pastor was summoned. He blessed the semiconscious man then Margot knelt by his side with a syringe in her hand. It only took a minute. Army Air Force Captain Winston Peters took the last train from London for a coveted rendezvous with his beloved wife of 49 years, Women's Auxiliary Army Corps NCO Victoria Peters.

Captain Winston Peters was laid to rest in Arlington National Cemetery beside NCO Victoria Peters.

The Pentagon cafeteria boasted a reputation as being one of the best eateries in Washington, DC. General Kurtz had taken Dutch Henry there for lunch.

"I'm sorry about Mister Peters. Your father-in-law was an outstanding gentleman."

"Thank you. The twins were very close to Winston. It's been hard for them. He was always with the girls after we got them back from those kidnappers."

"Thank God Cotton and Stroud were on the case."

"Damn right! I understand Mike was a Marine. Trudy and the kids are crazy about Cottonmouth."

"Ruth informed us about Stroud. I checked him out. Mike has a chestful of ribbons."

"I guess she told you about London."

"She said we don't have to worry about funding anymore, something to do with that Cayman Bank. She didn't offer many details. That so-called suicide sounds like a murder to me."

"I'd bet on it. Winston told me we only have a handful of operatives. If you and General Marshal can come up with a few more people, we have the money now to fund operations we weren't capable of in the past."

"I'll get with Jack and we'll put our heads together. Clinton has us involved in a civil war in Kosovo. I don't think we should be over there. Jack thinks it's a smoke screen for Monica Lewinsky, but there is some good news. Hungary, the Czech Republic, and Poland just joined NATO."

"That is good news. What's the story on Russia?"

"Not bad. Boris Yeltsin is a drunkard, but he's a peaceful man. The Premier is nothing like Nikita Khrushchev. Russia is not a threat now, at least for the time being. Red China is another matter."

"What's China up to?"

"The Chinese have been stealing our nuclear secrets for years. But Congress is such a bunch of pussies they refuse to do anything about it."

"Great representatives, aren't they?"

"And they get worse every fucking year."

"At least Rico's top dogs are onboard. That helps a lot."

General Kurtz laughed. "I never thought I'd be working with the Mafia."

Dutch nodded. "If it wasn't for Rico and Michael, my daughters would be dead. Those Arab fruitcakes are seriously fucked up."

"Ruth told me what Harry did with that Baz person. Harry has style."

"Harry's a pint-size version of Cottonmouth."

"Military Intelligence owes me a favor or two. I'll see if they can recommend somebody."

"Sounds swell, general. I'm flying out for London. I'll be back Saturday afternoon."

Chapter Fourteen

A Problem

Lydia held court while she and Uriah had a drink. "Scotland Yard's been keeping tabs on Osama bin Laden ever since 1979 when he was in Afghanistan helping the Mujahideen. We know his early schooling involved a crackpot teacher who believed in jihad and killing infidels. Charlie Wilson, a congressman from Texas, supplied the Afghans with Stinger missiles fronted by the CIA.

"During the war he built his Al Qaeda network with the men he served with in Afghanistan. The Russians lost the war then hightailed it home in '89. He returned to Saudi Arabia the big hero. That's when he dropped a clanger, speaking out against the Gulf War and the royal family's relationship with the Americans. The Saudis kicked him out in '92, and revoked his citizenship in '94. Then his father disowned the crazy thing. From Saudi Arabia he moved to Sudan, where his terrorist organization spread like a trollop's bum over a ten pound note. The Sudanese got word of his shenanigans, so they kicked him out in 1996.

He left Sudan, transporting his raghead ass back to Afghanistan where he set up those training camps.

"Al Qaeda has murdered thousands of innocent civilians, and blown up places all over the Middle East. They're responsible for those hotel bombings in Yemen, and two more bombing attacks in Saudi Arabia. They bombed the US embassies in Kenya and Tanzania. Mubarak was in Ethiopia when they tried to kill him. To top it off, the nutter declared war on the United States when he was kicked out of Sudan."

"Osama bin Laden is a damned *meshuggener*," Uriah declared.

Lydia continued. "Two years ago he and some other camel jocks formed a coalition they called the International Islamic Front for Jihad against the Jews. That included Al Qaeda, the Egyptian Islamic Jihad, the Egyptian Islamic Group, and two more sects in Kashmir and Bangladesh.

"Then they ran an ad in that London Arabic newspaper, *Al Quds Al Arabi*, calling on all Muslims to kill Americans and their friends, military or civilian. It makes no difference to those hooligan psychopaths."

"Know what, Lydia? I'd like to catch that string bean fuck and stuff a ham sandwich down his throat."

"If we catch him, Uriah, he'll eat the whole bloody pig!"

"Have you noticed when we're out we see Muslims drinking alcohol?"

"Yes, Allah's little hypocrites."

"I'll wager a fiver they order pork cassoulet when nobody's looking."

"You're a regular *Fawlty Towers*, you are."

"At your service, Miss Rumpy-Pumpy."

"Did the maps come yet?"

"Mossad delivered them last night."

General Marshal and General Kurtz were comparing intelligence reports with the Israeli maps Dutch Henry brought back from London.

"Bin Laden's big training camp is right about there. Our satellites confirm it. Too bad we can't send in a squadron of B-52s. They'd blow the damn thing straight up bin Laden's ass."

"Right and the UN would shit all over themselves. They'd start whining about international borders, those poor misunderstood Afghans, then the president would make a big weepy speech, and some idiot in Congress would leak all the names."

"The UN's about as useless as tits on a boar hog. And Congress couldn't find their ass in the dark with both hands," General Kurtz opined.

Dutch smiled. "Well, I see we're all in agreement."

The men chuckled. Then they began discussing ways into the valley and out again without getting their people killed.

General Kurtz continued. "Back in '78 two of Ross Perot's EDS executives got arrested in Iran by the Iranian Revolutionary Guard. Perot tried getting them out through diplomatic channels, but that didn't work. So he hired a retired Green Beret colonel to form a rescue operation. That man's name was Arthur Simons.

"Simons was able to pull it off after one of his people infiltrated the Iranian Guard. He incited a riot against the prison. Perot got inside and briefed his men on the situation. The rioters stormed the prison, and 12,000 prisoners were set free. Simons managed to get his group across the border into Turkey with the Guard in hot pursuit. What we need is an accomplice who doesn't give a shit about bin Laden or any of his jihad bullshit."

"You mean inside the camp?" General Marshal asked.

"No, not the camp. We need somebody on the ground. If we run into trouble, we might need a place to set down coming back out."

"Good idea."

"We have two men in Louisiana who fit the bill. Karl Musgrove was a pilot in Vietnam. They probably know somebody we could use. I'll call and ask."

⌒

"That's the target. Do you and Moses want the job?"

"It sounds dangerous as hell. What do we get for risking our necks?"

"I'm authorized to offer you one million dollars when you complete the mission."

"I'll get back to you in the morning, general."

Karl walked down to the pier where Blue Pony was fishing. "Wanna make a million bucks?"

"Sounds like we get ass shot off."

"We'd have all the money we'll ever need. You and I could leave his pest hole and live the life of Riley."

"What they want us to do?"

"Blow up a terrorist training camp in Afghanistan."

"Is that all?"

"Right, we could get our ass shot off."

"How we get in?"

"They haven't figured that out yet."

"You fly helicopters?"

"I can fly most planes up to four-engine jobs."

"How many men we need?"

"I don't know."

"What about nephew?"

"I don't want Billy in harm's way."

"Not Billy, Wanda. She flies choppers."

"That's even worse, Moses. What if she got hurt or killed?"

"Give them half of money."

"Hey, now that's a possibility."

"Keep money in family."

"Sure, but they're back on active duty."

"Ask general to get them furlough."

"He could swing that, all right."

"Find out how big place is. How many people live there."

"I'll fly up to Washington tomorrow. I don't trust these cell phones."

"I got uh bite."

His cork bobbed under. A minute later Moses landed a four-pound catfish for supper.

⌁

Zephyr was perplexed. She was experiencing something she didn't know how to deal with. It embarrassed her, making it difficult for her to discuss the matter with Zelda. Finally, in desperation, she broached the subject.

"I have a problem."

"What's wrong?"

"It's embarrassing."

"Tell me."

"I read about it in the *Ladies Home Journal*, how our hormones make us crazy sometimes. We have estrogen and testosterone in us. Mine seem to be running away with me. I'm … I'm horny!"

"Oh no! You're going to turn into a Knight Park floozy and ruin the family name."

"Stop teasing me. This isn't funny, okay."

"Doctor Johnson and I discussed this when I was pregnant with Jake. I felt that way about my fourth month. It's nature, Zephyr. The way men and women are put together. He told me if the feelings persisted to buy a vibrator. Thankfully mine went away before Jake was born."

"You haven't had it since then."

"Sometimes, on occasion, but not as intense as when I was pregnant."

"Did you get a vibrator?"

"No, it never got that serious with me."

"Well, it's driving me crazy. I pace the floor at night."

"Sounds like you need one pretty bad."

"I'd be too embarrassed to go in one of those places."

"I'll go with you."

The next day Zelda accompanied her sister to the adult book store in Sandy Springs. When they walked in, they saw books, videos, sexual devices, and lubricants everywhere they looked. Zephyr blushed and turned around to leave. Zelda took her by the arm, pulling her over to a large glass case where an assortment of vibrators was on display.

"That looks like a good one. You can pretend you're having sex with Tom Selleck."

"Oh stop it before someone hears you."

"It looks like those things with balls on the end are the kind you hold against you."

"I'm sure not sticking one of those pointy things in me."

"Some cream, maybe?"

"Goodness, no! I'm wet enough already."

"Imagine, my own big sister … what's a mother to do?"

"If you don't hush I'm gonna pinch your bottom!"

Zelda snickered, paid the cashier, and they left with a Ladies Home Companion.

That night when Zephyr was alone in her bedroom, she plugged it in. Within seconds, she experienced a breathtaking orgasm.

A few minutes later there was a knock at her door. "You did it, didn't you?

"How did you know?"

"I was downstairs with Mom and Dad having a glass of wine. I spilled white wine all over Jake and Gran-paw's couch. You nearly killed me!"

"You mean you had one too?"

"Yes! It was delightful. I had no idea."

"This is amazing."

"Poor Jake had wine in his hair."

"Do Mom and Dad suspect anything?"

"No. They thought I was just being clumsy."

Zephyr just shook her head, grinning sheepishly at her twin sister. Zelda laughed out loud. They had discovered a unique way to share their feminine secrets. Education and cheerleading had taken on a whole new perspective, especially after Zelda purchased her own Ladies Home Companion.

Chapter Fifteen

Secret Mission

George W. Bush became the forty-third US president following a 5-4 decision by the Supreme Court regarding the presidential election of 2000. Albert Gore won the popular vote. George Bush won the Electoral College. Florida became mired in political controversy with Bush winning by 1,800 votes out of a total cast by 6,000,000 Floridians. The all-Democrat Florida Supreme Court demanded a recount, which was denied by the United States Supreme Court. A recount with Democrats controlling the outcome was deemed unconstitutional. The Oval Office went to Bush. And the Left swelled up like a sick hop toad.

⤚

"You think we should?" Wanda asked her husband.

"An opportunity like this comes along once in a lifetime. What's troubling you?" Billy Ray asked.

"I couldn't stand it if you got killed."

"If we plan this right we'll be fine. Karl and Moses will be with us. And we'll get a half million dollars!"

"I know, but it still worries me. If we get shot down, then what?"

"That raghead camp is about 160 kilometers north of the Khyber Pass and Jalalabad. If we run into trouble, those CIA guys are a few miles east. They could be there in an hour or less."

"I know all that. But our base in Tajikistan is thirty minutes north. I don't trust those Pakistanis."

"Listen, we could organize a backup plan in both places."

"Now that idea I like. Maybe that's why I married you, smarty britches."

"You married me because I ring your bell like it was Easter Sunday."

"You are sooo bad! But you're half right, though."

"Which half?"

"You make me very happy, Billy Ray. You're sweet and kind and I love you for it."

"Sounds like you're up to something, Miss Wanda Jean."

"You catch on quick, Mister Billy Ray."

Wanda turned out the light, slipped out of her pajamas, and snuggled down beside Billy Ray in their comfy king-size bed.

⤶

"Mose, I think we oughta move the bank. We're gonna be gone four or five weeks. Some asshole's liable to come in here nosin' around and find it."

"Where you think?"

"I don't know. You got any suggestions?"

"Mister Gator, maybe?"

'Yeah, but where? That bastard's liable to eat one of us."

"Island behind gator got high bank. Him not climb up there."

"That might work. We can take your stepladder.

The two men set about digging up the Mason jars they had buried around the rose bushes. There were seven in all containing a little over $350,000 in cash. Seven packages had passed through the camp then out into the swamp where the alligator lived. Karl had purchased a plastic container in town. They placed their glass jars inside the plastic box, wrapping it with waterproof masking tape.

Down beside the pier Moses shot a carp feeding in the shallows. They pulled the fish into the bass boat and headed out. Twenty minutes later they were approaching the big reptile. In went the dead carp to distract the alligator. Blue Pony set up his stepladder and they scaled a four-foot embankment. The top of the grassy plateau was about 12,000 feet square. It rested on a sandstone foundation with an assortment of royal princess trees and azalea bushes mingled with ferns and angel oaks whose branches hung down to the surface of the ground.

"Wow! This place is really something."

"Good place for bank."

"It's like a fairyland. Good place for a hideout too."

"Under big tree. Keep guns and food in tent."

"I'll buy some survival rations when we get back. We could use this for an escape route."

"Get more bullets."

"Come on, that looks like a good spot up there."

The general decided on a single UH-1H Huey helicopter going in at 0300 while the terrorists were still asleep. An Apache was too much of a risk on a rogue assignment, in case the chopper went down. The Russians or Chinese would pay a fortune for that advanced computer technology.

Pakistan was ruled out as a backup. Their military had officers and enlisted personnel who were sympathetic with the Taliban. Revealing the assassination plot could jeopardize the mission.

The Huey was mounted with an M21 armament package on each

side of the aircraft. That consisted of a M134 minigun and a M158 seven-tube rocket launcher. An additional .50 caliber machine gun would be mounted inside each door. Wanda Jean would serve as pilot, and Karl Musgrove as copilot. Billy Ray and Moses Blue Pony were the door gunners.

General Kurtz stood in the doorway gazing out across the Panj River. He was thinking about the mission, and the three men and one very pretty woman he was sending out to kill Osama bin Laden. God help them if they fell into the hands of those Islamic butchers.

Their one story building had been constructed by the French in 1998 as part of a UN peacekeeping effort. Collapse of the Soviet Union in '91 had led to a five-year civil war between the Soviet-backed government and various rebel factions vying for control of the country. Chief among the antagonists were Islamic militants from Iran and Afghanistan intent on seizing control. Between 50,000 and 100,000 people had been killed in the fighting. An uneasy truce was finally established in 1999, with the independent Tajiks leaning toward Western Democracy.

"Your GPS has been programmed to guide you in. Stay down in the valleys, below the tops of those mountains. You don't want the Chinese or Iranians picking you up on radar. The camp is 31 miles due south. Take your time getting there. The moon will be full tonight so you'll be able to see well. When you start coming up on the camp, the valley will widen out. You'll see your first guard tower at the north end as you fly in. A second guard tower will be about 200 yards down on your left. A third tower will be at the far end of the compound. Moses, Billy Ray, you hit those towers while Wanda takes out the buildings."

"Head count, is that still the same?" Karl asked.

"Four hundred give or take a few."

"Go over that Mayday thing again, general, Wanda said."

"If you get into trouble and have to land, your distress call is 'grasshopper.' That's all you have to say to let me know you're down. Wanda is Number One, Karl is Number Two, Moses is Number Three, and Billy Ray is Number Four. Do not say your names over the radio. If you go down, we'll be there in a few minutes."

"You think bin Laden is still there?" Billy asked.

"Chatter is light coming from the camp, but it never has been very heavy. Intelligence believes he's there. My guess would be that small building beneath the middle guard tower. Those three buildings at the far end of the compound are the barracks. Your bad guys will be in there."

Wanda asked the general, "Do they have anything in those towers besides guns?"

"Machine guns and probably RPGs. Try and knock those out on your first pass."

Karl smiled at Wanda. "This should be a piece of cake."

"Don't underestimate your enemy," General Kurtz reminded them. "If bin Laden is there, those guards will be wide awake. Osama is their poster boy. They'll protect him with their lives."

"Need rifles if chopper goes down," Moses said."

"I thought of that. There's four AK-47s onboard and a crate of ammo. You have an extra canister for each machine gun. Those mini-guns have 4,000-round drums. That's about a minute's worth. Launch your rockets then get the hell out."

Karl looked at Blue Pony. "Moses, you got your lucky piece?"

"Mister Elephant in pocket."

General Kurtz stood. "Try and get some shut-eye. I'll wake you at 0200."

⌣

Lydia Sams had invited Uriah Frank over to her flat to relax and share a bottle of Boodles Gin. She had appropriated 15,000 pounds of their newfound wealth to decorate her place with new furniture, a new kitchen, new bath, and a nice paint color. Before doing so she asked

Uriah if he thought it would be appropriate to spend the money on her living quarters. Indeed it would, he told her. He praised her loyalty as an MI-6 operative, telling her she was worth every shilling.

"Do you like it? I made it girly so I can forget the things we do when I come home at night."

"It's you, Lydia, subtle but very attractive. You have excellent taste. I love what you've done with the place."

"I'm delighted you like it."

"You're a brave woman. I'm very fond of you …" Uriah stopped short, fearful he had overstepped their boundary of friendship.

Lydia saw his discomfort, so she changed the subject. "Your Knesset should never have given back the land Israel took in that first war with Lebanon. Syria is busy ratcheting up more terrorist attacks right now. So are the Palestinians and those crazy Iranians. Kofi Annan blew it as a UN Peacekeeper in Rwanda. Now he's doing the same thing again as Secretary-General."

"I know. Hezbollah kidnapped another one of our soldiers last week. They found him in the desert cut to pieces. Annan is a weak leader."

"Do they have any idea who did it?"

"All we know is that they came from Lebanon."

"That nest of vipers should be wiped out, every last one of them."

"Another air attack is in the works, as soon as Israel determines where most of them are hiding. It's hard, fighting an enemy that attacks then blends in with civilians. So many innocent people have been killed because of that. Hezbollah doesn't care, Al Qaeda, none of them give a rat's ass."

"I've never understood why so many people dislike the Jews. Why is that, Uriah?"

"Jews are clannish, close-knit. They're shrewd business people too. They'll haggle with you over a pound note. The majority believe Jesus was a prophet, not the son of God. And in most Jewish families the woman rules the household. Many of them have become secular leftists. Liberal beliefs are their new religion. They no longer follow the Torah."

"Do you believe in Jesus?"

"Yes, I'm a Christian Jew."

"You're a fine Christian Jew, Uriah. And you're a very handsome man."

"Thank you, Lydia. You're the bravest woman I've ever known, besides being perfectly gorgeous."

She touched his cheek, smiling. Then she took his hand. "I know how you feel about me, Uriah."

"I never meant to impose my feelings. I've tried very hard to be professional."

"It's all right, luv. Jolly good, because I feel the same way about you."

"Are you serious?"

"I was very worried when you went on that ship."

"It was touch and go for a few minutes."

"I would have come to rescue you if things had gone wonky."

"You're a wonder."

"I mean every word. You've become an important part of my life, you lovely man."

"Haven't other men been in love with you?"

"Lots of men asked me out, but I never made love with any of them. I always dreamed about a knight in shining armor who would love me and understand my work, Queen and country and all that. But it never happened, not until you came along.

"I respect your dedication and patience."

"So will you love and protect me forever?" She giggled, enjoying herself and the euphoria of being open with Uriah for the first time.

Uriah teased her back. "And will you love and protect me?"

"Yes, with all my heart. We'll make a smashing couple, Mister Frank."

They embraced, laughing and kissing. Lydia stood, unbuttoning her white blouse and placing it on a chair. She undid her brassiere and laid that on the chair. Then she shimmied out of her skirt and panties and sat down beside Uriah on her new linen sofa.

Uriah took a full breast in each hand, kissing her tender and swollen nipples. Lydia shuddered, reaching for the belt buckle on his trousers.

Chapter Sixteen

Wanda

"It looks like a big white ocean, doesn't it?"

"Yes, it's beautiful. The moon does wonders for places like this."

"Rocks and mountains, but where's all the trees?"

"Keep your eyes peeled. We're almost there."

"Up ahead. I see something."

They flew over a wooden cross with a man dangling from the crossbar. Several bodies lay on the ground. A dozen vultures took flight.

"Did you see that?"

"I saw it. They've been busy."

"I saw bones down there."

"God, you can smell it."

"People crazy, no damn good."

"Animals don't do shit like that, just these bastards."

"There's the first tower. I'm going in low."

Moses charged his weapon.

As Wanda flew past the guard tower, Blue Pony pulled the trigger. Planks and matting flew in all directions, and red sparks from the .50 caliber slugs striking the machine gun inside. A guard was blown out the backside of the twenty-foot structure.

Wanda zeroed in on the small building beneath the second tower. She fired. The roof of the building lifted in the air then erupted into a huge fireball. Wanda veered right to escape the debris field.

"That wasn't bin Laden. We hit an ammo dump."

"You think Intelligence fucked up?"

"Fuck Intelligence! Let's deal with what we got."

Tracers were streaking past the helicopter on both sides.

Bang! Bang!

Two rounds struck the fuselage. Wanda opened fire with her miniguns. The third guard tower disintegrated in a swirling cloud of smoke and flying timbers.

"Reef it around, Wanda. Hit those barracks."

Wanda lay the Huey over on its side, coming around for a pass at the barracks. She squeezed the trigger. Tracers were coming from the middle tower and all three buildings. The rear barracks exploded, hurling beams and wooden planks in the air. Then the second barracks went up. Bodies pinwheeled across the courtyard. Salvoing her final rockets, the front barracks exploded.

Bang! Bang! Bang!

Billy Ray and Moses were firing off their second canisters of .50 caliber ammunition. The 4,000-round minidrums were half empty.

"Billy! Get that middle tower!"

Bang! Bang!

"Karl! Take it …" Wanda slumped in her seat, losing consciousness.

Musgrove flew the Huey down to ground level then performed a 360 with the miniguns blazing.

"Billy Ray, get up here! Tend to Wanda!"

Musgrove tilted the nose of the chopper forward, giving it full throttle. They went soaring up the valley.

"Moses, help Billy. First-aid kits are behind the seats."

They got her out of the pilot's seat and down on the chopper floor. A bullet had punctured her right side. Wanda was bleeding from her nose and mouth.

"Turn facedown so not choke on blood."

Fighting back tears, Billy turned Wanda over on her stomach. The right side of her flight suit was soaked. The two men got her flight suit down to her waist.

"You think she'll be okay?"

Wanda looked dead in the moonlight.

"Great Spirit watch over Wanda now. Hold arm while I fix bandage."

Wanda coughed up a clot of blood. She took hold of her husband's hand pulling it against her cheek.

Karl smacked the fuel gauges. "Shit. They got our tanks. We can't make it. I'm calling base."

"Grasshopper … Grasshopper … Number One is down … Number One is down … Grasshopper … Send help pronto … Number One is down … Twenty miles out … Twenty miles out."

"I read you five by five … we're on the way."

The turboshaft engine backfired, twice, then twice again.

"We're outta go-juice. I'm taking her down."

The landing was rough.

"I smell gas. You two get Wanda outta here. I'll bring the guns and ammo."

Billy Ray and Blue Pony carried their unconscious cargo to a flat area well clear of the damaged Huey. Karl shucked off his flight suit, placing it over Billy Ray's suit to keep Wanda warm. The night air was cold in the Afghan mountains. Blue Pony ran back, setting the aircraft on fire.

"She looks bad, Karl. She looks real bad."

"Hang on, son. They'll be here in a minute."

Moses slipped his golden elephant charm from his breast pocket, placing it gently around Wanda's neck. In the distance they heard the *wop-wop-wop* of an approaching helicopter. Karl stood, waving his flashlight back and forth. As the second Huey came down to land, the men hovered over the woman shielding her from the prop wash of flying sand.

⌒

"What blood type is she?" the medic asked.

Billy wiped his tears. "She's O negative."

"Any you people O negative?"

General Kurtz answered. "I am. I'm O negative."

"She's almost bled out, sir. I have a manual infusion pump in my kit. I can use that to pump your blood into her vein. It's the only way I can save her, general."

"Then let's get on with it."

General Kurtz removed his Marine jacket and shirt and lay down beside Wanda on the deck of the aircraft. The young medic took out his pumping device and went to work.

They were flying at 110 knots toward Khorugh, a small city in Tajikistan with an adequate hospital facility. Billy Ray knelt down beside Wanda Jean and General Kurtz and prayed. Moses Blue Pony sat cross-legged on the other side of the prone figures reciting an ancient prayer taught him by an old medicine man. Karl Musgrove sat holding on to the side of the aircraft, staring down at his beleaguered friends.

⌒

They had her on a cloth-covered operating table with an oxygen mask over her face. A blood transfusion was inserted into her right arm. She was under anesthesia. There was a tube down her nose sucking out blood. Another tube was taped inside her wound, draining blood into a plastic pouch. A Russian doctor was explaining the procedure to the five men standing around the table.

"I have to open her chest to get to the problem. She has a severed artery. I can put a sleeve on that. The right lung is punctured on both sides. The bullet is lodged near the heart. I'll take the bullet out, patch up the lung, and she'll be good as new in a couple of months."

General Kurtz asked, "How many of these operations have you done, doctor?"

"I've performed five of these surgeries."

"Did your patients live?" Billy Ray was nervous.

"Four lived. One was hurt so badly he didn't make it. Chest surgery is not my specialty, but I am versed in the procedure. The head nurse assisting me has been involved with dozens of these operations. We're all veterans of these terrible wars, general."

General Kurtz moved toward the door. "If you need more blood, I'll be outside."

"Thank you, general. We have four pints in our refrigeration unit."

"You make her right. She fine warrior," Moses declared.

"It never hurts to pray, gentlemen."

Billy Ray leaned over Wanda Jean and kissed her lips. The four of them went outside to wait while the doctor and his nurses worked to save Wanda's life. General Kurtz began experiencing dizzy spells. Karl went down the corridor, searching for something for the general to eat. Billy Ray went with him. Blue Pony located an empty room with twin beds. He led the general inside, helped him off with his pants and shirt, and placed a blanket over his patient.

The pilot and copilot came in to get warm. Jones, the medic, was in the operating room observing the procedure. Their helicopter was secured on the lawn out front. The pilots had brought the weapons and ammunition box inside with them. Karl and Billy Ray were just coming down the hallway with a basket of food.

"Where's the general?"

Blue Pony stuck his head out the door. "I put general in bed."

"Come out here and eat something," Karl invited. "I got bananas, cornbread, goat cheese. And lookie here. Some kinda moonshine. It's strong as hell, but it goes down okay. Take a slug, son."

Billy Ray turned the quart container up and swallowed. "Damn! That stuff's awful.

"Blue Pony reached for the jug. "I got good feeling. I drink to Wanda."

Each in turn drank to Wanda Jean. An hour later they were all in better spirits. One of the nurses had stepped out with a positive report. They'd gotten the bullet out and repaired the artery. The medical team was still working on Wanda's chest.

General Kurtz appeared in the doorway in his USMC T-shirt and boxer shorts. "Did somebody mention alcohol?"

"Right here, general. We saved this for ya."

Kurtz turned the jar up and took a long pull. He wiped his mouth then turned to Billy Ray. "How's she doing?"

"The nurse told us she's gonna make it. I owe you, sir. Your transfusion saved Wanda's life."

"I'm in your debt, Billy. The four of you performed an extraordinary feat of courage. I'm indebted to each one of you. You make a hell of a team."

"When will we know about bin Laden, sir?"

"I'll check on it when we get back. That helicopter might attract attention. Somebody needs to be on the roof."

Blue Pony volunteered. "I'll go."

Karl stood. "I'll go with Moses. He can watch the chopper. I'll watch out back."

"It's cold out there. We'll spell you in an hour," General Kurtz told them.

⤳

"There's a shindig at the country club tonight. They have a live band, dinner, dancing. You girls want to go?" Dutch asked the twins.

"That might be fun." Zephyr looked at her sister.

"Would it be all right to bring Jake along or do I need a babysitter?" Zelda asked.

Trudy was a proud grandmother. "We can all take turns with Jakey Pooh. He likes music."

"Get ready, then. Dinner at eight. We'll leave here about 7:30."

It took them five minutes to reach the West Paces Ferry club and park the big Buick. Winston had left the majority of his estate to Trudy, one million dollars to Dutch, and $500,000 in escrow for each twin on their twenty-first birthday.

Most of Atlanta's Buckhead society was present for 1940s Night. The World War II veterans and their wives were eager to hear the old songs.

Dinner was served, and the band began to play. "Star Dust" was their first number. Trudy and Dutch got up to dance. Jake sat mesmerized in his highchair, watching the dancers and listening to the music.

"I want to dance too, Mommy."

"All right, you place your feet on top of mine, and I'll dance you around the floor."

Jake did as he was told and away they went. Several of the club members waved and smiled as Zelda and Jake danced by.

"You're a good dancer, Mommy."

The number came to an end, and they headed back to their table. Zelda paused to say hello to the club president and his charming wife. Just then the neighborhood gossip made her appearance, bustling up to the foursome standing at the edge of the dance floor. Aunt Pittypat, she was not.

"What a lovely little boy, and such dark skin."

"Why thank you. Jake is a little dark."

"Indeed, I bet his father was dark too."

It was then Zelda remembered what people had told her about the gossipy old woman, and her mean-spirited ways of always seeking out the worst in people. It was obvious she was trying to score points with the president and his wife.

"Now that you mention it, he was dark, quite dark."

Suspecting she had breached Zelda's defenses, the old woman went on with her suspicions about a "darkie in the woodpile." In truth, Zelda had just set the hook.

"Is he local, does he work around here, what does your husband do, girl?"

"I don't have a husband."

Eyeing Zelda suspiciously the old biddy exclaimed in an accusatory tone, sensing here might be an out-of-wedlock birth. "My word, young lady! You have no husband?"

"No, ma'am, I have no husband. We killed him!"

The gossip changed colors like a chameleon. First she blanched white, then she turned bright red, then she began sputtering like she'd swallowed a fish bone.

"Oh my! Oh my!"

Off she went, bustling away with her tail between her legs like a frightened canine being chased by an angry pussycat.

The president leaned over and whispered, "Well done, Zelda. Well done!"

From then until Jake's bedtime, Zelda and Jake danced the night away. She never mentioned the episode to her family. Zelda was at peace with the world. There was no shame or remorse. Zelda loved her little boy with all her heart.

The woman opened her eyes. She was in a comfortable but unfamiliar bed. The room was dark. She'd been having a strange dream about trying to get to Chattanooga, but she didn't have a car and no money to spend. She was out on the highway trying to catch a ride, but no automobiles would stop to give her a lift. Somehow she got lost. There were lots of strangers on the road, factory workers it seemed. And one old man who was standing in a ditch full of water. He seemed to like being in the water. It was depressing. She became concerned about finding her way back home again.

The woman heard a noise. Someone was there. "Hello?"

A shadow rose up, the lights switched on. Wanda stared in bewilderment at an array of faces then began to cry.

"I'm so happy … you're all alive."

"Don't cry, honey," Billy Ray warned her. "You've got stitches."

"Yes, you be still now," Blue Pony cautioned.

Karl and General Kurtz added their voices.

"Welcome back, Wanda Jean."

"Thank God you're all right!"

Even the medic was there. "The doctor told us you're going to mend nicely."

The men gathered around her bed. It resembled a family reunion. She had a tube down her nose, a morphine drip in her arm, and a catheter under the sheets.

"I think I remember getting shot. After that it's just a blank."

"We almost lost you," Billy Ray told her. "The medic here and General Kurtz saved your life."

"What happened?"

General Kurtz spoke up. "You and I have the same blood type, young lady. I gave you some of mine."

"They cut me open, didn't they? I can feel the bandages."

"It was the only way to get the bullet out and patch you up inside."

"Mister Elephant help too."

Wanda touched the golden charm around her neck. Tears leaked out both sides of her lashes. "I'm the luckiest girl in the world. I love each one of you wonderful men."

The copilot opened the door. "General, I think you better come take a look at this."

On the roof, the chopper pilot handed the general a pair of field binoculars. "Up there, sir, on the ridge."

"Damn it to hell! Looks like word got out about the raid."

"Sir, if we get in the air we'll stand a better chance. We got M-60s in both doors."

"We have four rifles downstairs. They can use those up here on the roof."

"Who'll operate the machine guns, general?"

"Me and Blue Pony. The others can defend the hospital."

"We better get started, sir. They'll be down here in a few minutes."

Back downstairs General Kurtz laid out the situation. Thirty or forty Al Qaeda were coming down the mountain. It appeared they knew about the raid, and presumably about Americans being inside the hospital. The Russian doctor voiced concern over his patients and his nurses.

The head nurse stepped forward. "I fought with my comrades in Afghanistan, and before that in the Crimea. Give me one of your weapons. I want to help you."

Another nurse spoke up, a small blonde woman. "I used to hunt game for the army. I know how to use a rifle."

"Karl, Billy Ray, there's your infantry unit. Moses and I will try to head them off from the air. If we fail, it'll be up to you two and these brave ladies here. Here, doctor, you take my .45. Good luck, all of you!"

"Sir, if things go badly … it's been real, sir."

"Same here, Billy. You too, Karl. Take care of the doctor and these nurses."

Karl, Billy Ray, and the two volunteers stood on the roof, watching as the helicopter lifted into the air. Moments later there was gunfire, both from the aircraft and Al Qaeda on the ground. The men and women looked on as tracers flew back and forth. Dust rose from the hillside where the M-60s plowed into the earth and ground cover. Now and then there were flashes as enemy rounds struck the helicopter.

Chapter Seventeen

A Time To Die

George Brown was studying a CIA dossier on one of the Russian diplomats in Washington, DC. His wife, Ruth Townsend, was upstairs using a secure satellite to call General Kurtz on his cell phone in Tajikistan. They hadn't been able to raise him in nearly four days. The raid had missed bin Laden, but nearly 300 of his followers had been killed and the terrorist camp destroyed.

"I don't like it, George. Our people always report in within twenty-four hours."

"His cell phone could be on the blink. Maybe he's down in a valley. No reception there, you know."

"Three and a half days? I don't think so."

"What do you propose we do?"

"I think we should contact Flanagan in Pakistan."

"You're probably right. I'll send out the Noah's Ark code."

That night a coded message was received via the special transmitter the two agents had hidden away in their townhouse on Churchill Road.

"Whereabouts Unknown. Request Instructions."

Ruth relayed a message back: "Find Him."

⌒

Karl Musgrove was pointing at the sky, cursing a blue streak. "Goddamn Murdering Sand Niggers!"

The helicopter had just spun out of control, round and round it went. Then it hit the ground. The next minute it began to burn.

Billy Ray shook his fist, venting his rage. "You filthy raghead butchers!"

"Billy Ray! Help the women get their defenses set up."

Karl ran down the stairs to bring up the box of Kalashnikov ammunition. When he pried off the wooden lid the rounds were sealed in small cardboard packets. They'd have to load each bullet by hand.

"Goddamn it, anyway!"

"Karl, we can take turns firing while the other man loads. The nurses said that's how they did it fighting the Russians."

"I better spread these around. Those sons a bitches! I wish we had some grenades."

"They got a truck out back. I can make some Molotov cocktails."

"Good idea! Tell the others to barricade the doors and windows."

The gas tanks on the helicopter exploded, sending up an orange ball of fire. Karl stood on the hospital roof gazing out across the Tajikistan landscape, thinking about the four brave men inside. He wondered if his friend and the others had been killed in the crash or if they had burned to death. He felt pangs of anger and guilt that he wasn't out there with them.

Oisha, the head nurse, came over to console her friend. She knew the sadness of losing one's comrades in war.

A few minutes later, they spied movement across the field.

"Somebody's coming!"

Three figures emerged from the trees on the far side of the hospital green.

"They're ours! They're ours!"

Karl raced down the stairs, clearing away the chairs and tables blocking the entranceway. He swung open the doors.

"Man, am I glad to see you guys! I thought you were toast!"

Blue Pony was following close behind the general with the copilot draped over his shoulders. General Kurtz was limping, using a tree limb for support. He had loops of bandoliers strung around his neck. The pilot was lugging three AK rifles and a full satchel of magazines.

"We got some uh the bastards. Jerry broke his ankle. I sprained my knee. What's new here?" General Kurtz asked.

"These nurses are A-OK," said Billy. "They're set up and ready to go."

"That's excellent! We need them."

"We got one crate of ammunition and four rifles, and some gasoline bombs." Karl pointed at the satchel. "That what I think it is, captain?"

Captain Waskow nodded. "AK magazines. We came down in our own kill zone."

Karl grinned. "Well that was a blessing in disguise."

"We radioed Pakistan," General Kurtz said. "They monitor the local traffic. An army of Al Qaeda is headed our way. They know we're here. Ruth Townsend knows we're here too."

"How many gas bombs did you make, Billy Ray?"

"I got seven."

"Any gasoline left?"

"There's enough for one or two more."

"There's a police building in town," Oisha said. "Some guns might be there."

"You and Karl go look," General Kurtz told them. "Watch out for those Arab monkeys. We didn't get 'em all."

⌣

The streets were empty. People had hurried indoors when they heard all the gunfire. The Al Qaeda survivors were tending their wounded back in the trees, waiting for reinforcements.

"Are you married, Karl?" Oisha asked.

"No, that ended a long time ago."

"I like you."

"I like you too, but you picked a hell of a time to talk romance."

"Now is good time. Tomorrow may not be here for us."

"Let's hope that don't happen."

"I think we live. Then I make love with you."

"You have an odd sense of courtship, lady."

"You are manly man. Courtship is good time. Over there, that's the building."

The jail was a three-room affair, with a desk and three chairs out front, another room with a heavily reinforced door and two army cots, and a third room that was locked. Musgrove kicked open the door. Inside they found a long workbench piled with Mauser rifles. Sitting on a separate table was a World War II MG-42 machine gun. Crates of ammunition were stacked around the walls.

"You know what this is, Oisha?"

"No."

"Looks like the armory for the local militia."

"My people don't like the crazy ones."

"We'll take the machine gun and a few rifles. Leave the rest in case your people decide to fight."

General Kurtz was on the hospital roof talking with the blonde nurse when he saw Oisha and Karl coming up the street. They were pulling a wagon behind them. He and Blondie hailed the pair when they spotted the machine gun. Blue Pony came running up the stairs to see what all the yelling was about.

"Down there, look."

"Great Spirit good to us. I go help."

◠

"How you feeling?"

"Much better, thank you."

"Does your chest hurt much?"

"Some, but not too bad."

"The doctor says you have to stay in bed awhile."

"I heard them talking. I know there's trouble."

"I'll protect you."

"I know, dear. I know what they'll do if they break in here too."

"Karl found a machine gun. The general says we have a good chance now."

"Don't let them take me alive, Billy."

Tears leaked down Billy's cheeks. He reached for Wanda's hand. "If it comes to that, I promise. I won't let them get you."

"I love you very much, Billy Ray Donavan."

"I wish I'd never gotten you mixed up in this."

"Hey, I liked the sound of all that money too."

"You deserve better, Wanda."

"I got what I wanted. I got you, Billy."

"If we get out of this alive, let's go somewhere on a vacation."

"What about our military obligations?"

"The general can fix it."

"I always wanted to see Paris and Rome."

"We'll go for a month, two months if you like."

"And be typical tourists, and take typical tours to all those touristy places."

"And drink wine, and eat tasty food, and have a second honeymoon."

"Tell me, how bad is it outside?"

"Washington's been alerted. We have plenty of weapons. We're supposed to get help from our CIA friends in Pakistan. They should be here anytime now."

"I hope so. That man that got hurt, is he okay?"

"The doctor fixed him up. He's on a walker, but he can fight."

"Have you got enough guns to leave me one?"

"Sure, I'll prop mine right here beside the bed."

The medic knocked on the door, then stuck his head inside. "The general wants us up top, Billy."

From the rooftop they observed a tall, bearded man wearing fatigues and holding a pistol. An elderly white-haired man was kneeling on the grass in front of the bearded man. Behind him was another village elder, held hostage by a second Al Qaeda.

"Americans! You come out now. We spare this old man."

"That bastard speaks English." Waskow sounded surprised.

"Sir, they won't spare shit. They'll kill us all."

"I know, Billy. Maybe I can save the old fellow. Come on over. Let's talk," he shouted.

"No! You come out. You come out or old man dies."

"There's no need for that. Come over here. Let's parlay."

"No! You come out now!"

"Talk to me, sir. We'll negotiate a peace."

Bang! Al Qaeda shot the old man in the back of his head.

Crack! Al Qaeda's head exploded.

Crack! The Al Qaeda behind him sprawled backward, mortally wounded.

The second village elder ran into the trees.

"My God, Oisha, that's good shooting!"

"You don't negotiate with madmen, Karl, you kill them. That's all they understand."

Moses smiled at Oisha. "I like the way you negotiate."

A barrage of gunfire erupted. Pieces of wood and plaster flew from the building. Broken glass fell to the ground and inside the structure.

"Stay down! Let 'em waste their ammunition," General Kurtz ordered.

The firing lasted several minutes then stopped. An afternoon sun was beginning to set behind the mountains. A cold chill was in the night air.

"When it gets dark they'll attack," General Kurtz said quietly. "They don't know we have automatic weapons. That's when we'll blast their ass. How many bombs you got, Billy?"

"Nine, sir."

"Spread 'em around the parapet."

"What about the machine gun, sir?" Waskow asked.

"That's our ace in the hole. We'll catch 'em off guard when they least expect it."

"I'll handle the machine gun, general."

"Roger that, Karl. The German 42 has a rapid rate of fire. You'll have to let it cool down after two or three belts."

"Maybe I pour water on barrel?" Moses suggested.

"If they mount a charge, yes, do that."

"You think help is still coming, sir?" the copilot asked.

"The CIA boys said they'd be here."

"They're sure as hell taking their sweet-ass time," Karl observed sourly.

"You men spread out. Wait for my signal. Doctor you go downstairs and turn off the lights. No, wait, get your patients moved first. Put everyone in the end of the building with Wanda Donavan."

∽

"Our people are in trouble, George, and all we get from Pakistan are weather reports. I'm sick and tired of their goddamned excuses. We need to do something NOW!"

"Ruth, they can't get airborne in a sandstorm. We need to think of something else."

"I know that, but what?

"Let me think a minute. Our flattops are out of the question. France is no good. Hmm. Africa would require a chain of command. What about London?"

"Call them. We're running out of time."

"I'm on my way, your ladyship."

The moon shone down on Khorugh. Mountains surrounding the village appeared as great mounds of platinum shimmering in the moonlight. Two hundred Al Qaeda soldiers waited in the trees across the road from the entrance to the hospital. Ten lone individuals waited nervously on the rooftop: a Russian physician, two Tajik nurses, and seven Americans. The Muslims viewed the American presence as an affront to Islam and to their leader, Osama bin Laden. Overhead a million stars twinkled in a black velvet sky. The voices of wolves could be heard drifting down the valley on the cold night air.

"Animal spirits honor us tonight."

"Red Man's mojo, general, beats the hell outta that Mohammad son of a bitch."

"I put bad mojo on Al Qaeda."

General Kurtz agreed. "Now you're talkin'."

"Sir, something's happening out there," Billy Ray warned.

The foliage was moving. A number of Al Qaeda had tied bushes around their bodies to look like part of the landscape. Glints on their rifles from the moon gave them away.

"Wait 'til they get closer. When I give the signal, unload on the bastards."

Seconds ticked by.

Billy Ray was anxious; Wanda was downstairs, fresh out of open heart surgery. General Kurtz was worried whether or not they could hold out long enough for reinforcements to arrive; the odds favored Al

Qaeda. Moses Blue Pony was thinking about a story told him by the old medicine man, about an Indian brave who was killed at Wounded Knee. He became a man-spirit and flew away from earth on the back of an eagle. The eagle took him to the Valley of the Moon where the beautiful Moon Princess lived.

"NOW!"

Seven Kalashnikovs and three Mauser rifles opened fire. A number of Al Qaeda fell. A firestorm of gunfire slammed into the stucco and frame building. The men and women on the rooftop huddled in the dark behind their protective barrier. Bits and pieces of the parapet began to crumble and fall away.

BOOM!

An RPG blew a hole in the middle section.

Billy Ray hurled two gasoline bombs. Several fanatics burst into flame.

BOOM!

A second RPG blasted a gaping hole between Blue Pony and General Kurtz. A third RPG missed, sailing harmlessly overhead.

"Hit 'em again!" General Kurtz barked.

Billy hurled another gasoline bomb … more screaming. Blondie fell backward, a bullet through her head. Blue Pony caught a round through his shoulder. More Al Qaeda went down.

"Downstairs! Get off the roof!"

Karl grabbed up the machine gun. Oisha was right behind him, lugging four canisters of ammunition with three belts draped around her neck. Downstairs they cleared away the chairs and tables blocking the front door. Karl set up the machine gun inside the hallway. Oisha knelt by his side ready to feed the sinister-looking weapon. Others waited in the dark with their rifles pointed toward the entranceway.

The door edged open an inch, then a few more inches. Suddenly, it burst open. A dozen Al Qaeda stormed the entrance. A sheet of orange flame greeted them with twenty 7.92mm rounds per second. The first belt was gone in less than a minute.

An RPG sailed through the doorway, exploding against the back wall. Another RPG hit the doorframe, blasting the right-hand door off its hinges.

Blue pony was pouring water over the smoldering gun barrel. Steam hissed from the weapon, filling the room with a metallic-smelling fog. Blue Pony ran for another pitcher. Flashes from the guns gave the water vapor a surreal pink effect. Al Qaeda dead were piling up in the doorway. The MG-42 was tearing their bodies to pieces as more fanatics stormed the building.

The fate of those in the hospital now hung by a thread.

The bolt clicked empty. Billy Ray had squeezed off his last round. It felt like a dream, a hideous nightmare. Everything dissolved into slow motion. Numb with fear, he dropped his weapon to the floor, wandering down the hallway, that last mile into eternity. They would not take his wife alive. He had promised her that. And it was breaking his heart.

He opened her door and walked inside the room. From the look on his face, she knew.

"We're almost out of bullets. They'll be in the building in a few minutes."

"Billy, I'm afraid."

"I am too, honey. I won't let them take you."

He sat down on the side of the bed, holding his wife's hand. They both had tears in their eyes.

The rifle he left earlier rested against the wall beside Wanda's bed.

KA-WHOOOM!

The world tilted, pans and bottles fell. They heard debris landing on top of the building.

Then another loud explosion farther away. Then close again, then from the road, then across the lawn at the base of the mountain. The building shook with each quaking blast. Bombs and rockets rained down like God's own deliverance. Men were blown to pieces.

The door flew open. "Billy, it's the Israelis. They sent planes. We're saved!"

The bombardment went on for what seemed like an eternity, in reality no more than twenty minutes. One last strafing run and they flew away over the mountains.

The carnage was devastating. The building was a shambles. The remaining Al Qaeda were retreating into the hills.

Karl Musgrove lay on his back behind the smoldering machine gun, his forearm over his eyes. Oisha was sprawled across his chest. In death, they appeared as lovers.

The doctor was tending to Blue Pony who had been hit a second and third time.

Jerry, the copilot was dead. The medic had been killed trying to help Jerry.

Blondie was dead on the roof. She and Oisha would be honored as heroines by their village. Their fame would spread throughout the Gorno-Badakhshan Province, and far beyond the mountains.

General Kurtz and Captain Waskow waited their turn with flesh wounds.

They heard a helicopter landing out front.

～

The chopper pilot saluted General Kurtz. "I'm sorry we're late, sir. A sandstorm had us socked in."

"Understood. How did Israel know about us?"

"I don't know, sir. The storm began lifting last night. We received a call from London around 2100 hours to stand down until 0700 this morning. No explanation was given. We took off around 0530 then waited in the hills about ten miles from here. That's when we heard the bombing. When it stopped we came on in."

"I want to take Jerry back with me," Captain Waskow told the two men.

"We can take them all, sir."

"General, if I make a list can you have supplies flown in?" the doctor asked. "I'm not going to abandon these people. We have another hospital to build."

"Write everything down, doc. I'll see to it personally."

"I take Karl home?" Moses Blue Pony's voice was sad.

"Of course you can. We'll bury Karl in Arlington if that's what you want."

Billy Ray knelt down beside his uncle and Oisha. He felt relief knowing Wanda was safe and the fighting was over, but he also felt the grim reality that an important part of his life was dead and gone forever. Uncle Karl had been like a father to him ever since he was a boy. He would miss Karl Musgrove a great deal. So would Moses Blue Pony.

Chapter Eighteen

September 2001

Uriah Frank was grateful his country had acted against Al Qaeda. But he felt disappointment that they didn't get there in time to save everyone. Getting the go-ahead from the top brass had taken hours. Then a tanker plane had to be dispatched before the F-15s could be scrambled. Five of the ten had been saved plus the patients and nurses in the hospital.

"The general called this morning. He asked me to thank everyone that helped.

"You did your job, Uriah. Your laddies saved the day."

"I can't imagine being captured, can you?"

"I'd put a bullet through me noggin. Getting raped then cut up like a bloody hen, no thank you."

"They were stoning people back when Christ walked the streets of Jerusalem. Remember when Jesus told His parable about casting the first stone? Muslims haven't advanced a lick in 2,000 years."

"I'm proud of you, Boo. Let's go to our place and get ourselves proper wobbly."

Their place was an old English pub seldom visited by the tourists, but quite suitable for locals. English businessmen went there to drink and discuss contracts. There were soldiers, blue collars, and volumes of secretaries. The proprietor was a leftover from World War II. He was bent and shaggy with a weather-beaten face, but he loved Lydia, who always gave him a peck on the cheek. The barmaid, Maggie, the proprietor's wife, treated the young couple like her own son and daughter.

"Blimey, tha two uh ya look fagged-out. A pint of bitters will lift the ole spirits, it will."

"Maggie, you're a sweetheart."

"Been workin' hard, 'ave we?"

"Yes, ma'am. Night 'n' day."

Maggie wandered over to the bar to fetch their drinks. Upon her return she complimented Lydia.

"I was a wee lass like yerself once, pretty 'n' proper. Then old froggie over there up an' stole me ladyship. That was back in '44. I had me a job weldin' airplanes, I did. Along 'e comes one fine day with 'is crafty talk an' stole me heart right out from under me gizzard. 'E never give it back, did 'e?"

"Do you mind so?"

Some of the woman's accent faded. "If I had it to do over again I wouldn't change a thing, not one. Those war years, we barely had food on the table. Mister Churchill pulled us through all right, God bless 'is soul. I got no complaints. Old froggie is a good un, 'e is." Maggie left to tend to her other customers.

An hour later they were well into their third pint of bitters.

"You think we'll be like them in fifty years, Boo?"

"You'll outlive me, Lydia."

"Why do you say that?"

"Because you like it too much. I won't last fifty years."

"Get back! You like it just as much as I do."

"Yes, but I do most of the work."

"Next time you stay downstairs. I'll mount the throne."

"It's been three days."

"Don't start talkin' yer trash. I'll soil me knickers."

"Remember our first time, when you pulled off all your clothes?"

"Don't remind me. You'll get me all wet."

"And you got on top. And nearly fainted when you lost your cookies?"

"You're making me horny, Uriah."

"And how you talk that East End cockney when we're pounding the mattress together?"

"Stop it. I'm getting soaked."

He placed his hand under the table, gently sliding his fingers along her inner thigh, caressing her blue undergarment.

"Then right before you climax you shudder, all urgent-like, grabbing me and holding on tight."

"Boo, you're making me crazy."

"I'm crazy about you, Lydia Sams."

"Take me home! I'm gagging for it!"

⌇

Moses Blue Pony was sitting on his front porch with his two dogs and Swamp Kat. The sun was going down over the bayou. That was his favorite time of day. He'd bought himself a bug zapper to kill the gnats and mosquitoes. Every few seconds another insect blundered into the glowing trap.

Karl Musgrove might have laughed at all the fuss and bother that went into his interment in Arlington National Cemetery. But he would have been proud of the people who came to tell him goodbye: General Kurtz, Ruth Townsend and George Brown, Rico, Dutch Henry, General

Marshal, and Billy Ray and Wanda Jean. There were others but those were the people he respected most—and Moses Blue Pony.

The old cat sat beside him on the couch gazing out into the twilight. Lightning bugs appeared. The frogs began serenading one another. Up in the treetops a pair of owls hooted back and forth. Moses was remembering the happy times he and Karl shared together. He missed his friend. Even the animals seemed to understand that something was missing.

In the distance a pair of headlights appeared, bouncing down the rutted trail to the cabin. Moses went inside, taking down his 12 gauge Ithaca pump, then returned to his couch and waited with the dogs and his cat. A black Humvee pulled up in front of the cabin.

"Are you Moses Blue Pony?"

"Who wants me?"

"Mike Stroud. I'm friends of Townsend and Brown."

"Come on up. White Devil won't bite."

Stroud got out of his vehicle, walked up to the porch, and sat down on the front stoop.

"I've heard a lot of good things about you, Moses. They tell me you're a spirit walker. They say you're a good man in a fight."

"People say many things."

"General Kurtz called you the perfect soldier."

"What you want?"

"They said we might work together as partners."

"People tell you bullshit."

"I don't think so."

"I had partner. Him dead now."

"I know. That's why we want you to stay with the group."

"You talk crazy. I got ass shot off. They want more?"

"That's right. They want more."

"Maybe I shoot your ass off."

"You're no murderer, but you are a patriot."

Moses sat eyeing the stranger on his stoop. He was angular and big, a strong man with the eyes of a hunter. There were worry lines around his eyes and mouth. He saw in Stroud a faint resemblance to his friend, Karl Musgrove. Moses laid his shotgun on the couch and slowly stood up. There was still pain from the gunshot wounds.

"You want whiskey?"

"Sure, I'd like a drink."

Moses brought out a bottle of Old Grand-Dad, a bowl of ice, and two wooden mugs.

They talked into the night, about their tours of duty in Vietnam, about the state of the world and its many problems. And about the people they'd worked with and liked.

"Why you get involved with these people?" Moses asked.

"I guess I'm a sucker for the underdog, Moses. The whole fucking world is an underdog. We got political scumbags on Capitol Hill, and Muslim scumbags all over the Middle East. Communist scumbags in North Korea and China, white-collar scumbags on Wall Street, and that ass-wipe herd uh pukes up at the UN. The Shit River never stops, and it flows downhill."

"What I got to do to be partner."

"I asked Ruth Townsend that same question two months ago. That's when I decided to go all in. You know what she said?"

"No."

"Ruth told me the United States might not survive unless regular folks start stepping up to the plate. It took me a while to get that through my thick head. She's right, you know. "

"How can so few make difference?"

"I asked Ruth that question too"

"What she tell you?"

"Ruth told me Spartacus whipped the Roman Legions with an army of slaves. King Richard beat Saladin at Jaffa with a smaller force. Old Hickory defeated the British in New Orleans. The outnumbered

Brits fought off the Luftwaffe, and we sank four Jap carriers at Midway, against all the odds. Ruth said those of us who get killed are heroes. 'Plant the seeds of freedom,' she said."

"Ruth savvy woman. We sleep on it. Go to town in morning for breakfast."

"Before I forget, I brought you something."

Stroud went out to the Humvee. He brought back a suitcase tied with a blue ribbon.

"What you bring me?"

"Open it, Moses."

Moses untied the ribbon and opened the suitcase. Inside was $500,000 in one hundred dollar bills, his and Karl's reward for the Afghan raid.

September 2001

8:46 a.m.: American Airlines Flight 11, flown by Al Qaeda hijacker Mohammad Atta, flew into the North Tower of the World Trade Center, exploding and creating a massive fire inside the building. All 92 passengers and the crew were killed instantly. The Boeing 767 struck the North Tower between the 94rd and 98th floors at approximately 470 miles per hour with about 20,000 gallons of jet fuel onboard. All elevators and stairwells were rendered impassable on impact, trapping 1,355 people above the fire.

9:03 a.m.: United Airlines Flight 175, another Boeing 767, piloted by Al Qaeda Marwan al-Shehhi, slammed into the South Tower between the 77th and 85th floors at roughly 590 miles per hour. It, too, carried approximately 20,000 gallons of jet fuel. All 51 passengers and nine crew members perished instantly. A lot of people were above the impact area, but one stairwell survived the crash and remained open. Six hundred unfortunate souls were never aware of the open escape route.

9:01 a.m.: Ruth Townsend's cell phone rang. She was standing in the lounge at CIA headquarters watching the drama unfold on a television screen. Her husband was out of town on official business.

"Ruth, are you watching the news?"

"Yes, George. We're all just stunned. Where are you?"

"I'm at Wild Blue in the North Tower."

"Oh my God! Can you get out?"

"No! Everything's blocked. I've tried."

"Is the fire department there yet?"

"Not yet. There's a lot of people here with me."

"Can you get to the roof?"

"That won't work either. The rising heat and all the smoke would wreck a helicopter."

"My God, surely something can be done."

"We're doing our best. The smoke is really bad."

"Christ … I wish … I want to help you."

"Pray for us, Ruth. Please pray for us. I'll get back to you in a few minutes."

The line went dead. Ruth rushed into the ladies room and threw up.

9:37 a.m.: American Airlines Flight 77, a Boeing 757 flown by Al Qaeda Hani Hanjour, flew into the western wall of the Pentagon, creating a deadly inferno. Fifty-three passengers and six crew members died, plus 125 people inside the building.

10:03 a.m.: United Airlines Flight 93, a second Boeing 757, crashed upside down in a field near Shanksville, Pennsylvania. Thirty-three passengers, plus a crew of seven, were killed.

Just before the crash of Flight 93, Thomas Burnett Jr. told his wife over his cell phone: "I know we're all going to die. There's three of us who's going to do something about it. I love you, honey."

Todd Beamer was heard over an open line: "Are you guys ready? Let's roll."

Sandy Bradshaw, a flight attendant, called her husband, explaining that she had slipped into a galley and was filling pitchers with boiling water. Her last words to her husband: "Everyone's running to first class. I've got to go. 'Bye."

⛳

Heat rising from the fires through the elevator shafts, stairwells, and the floors themselves were turning the upper levels into ovens. Those trapped were drenched with sweat. It was difficult to breathe. Facing one's own mortality was taking a heavy toll.

9:21 a.m.: "Ruth, listen to me. It's really bad here." *Coughing* "They can't get to us." *Coughing* "Do you remember where the insurance policies are?"

Ruth, weeping. "Yes, George. I remember. Please … are the stairs all blocked?"

"We can't get out. It's too hot … we're done for."

"I love you so much. Please don't die. Please."

"I love you, Ruth. I always loved you."

"George … George …" Ruth sobbed.

She could hear her husband's labored breathing. People were crying.

"I have to … window …"

She heard loud noises … glass falling … screaming. "George! Answer Me!"

"Goodbye, my darling."

George Brown jumped from the 106th floor of the North Tower when the searing heat and suffocating smoke became unbearable. His plunge lasted nearly 13 seconds.

9:59 a.m.: South Tower collapsed
10:28 a.m.: North Tower collapsed.

⌒

Mike Stroud returned home emotionally and physically exhausted. It had been a rotten-ass day. September 11, 2001, was an absolute horror show. He jumped when he saw a figure sitting on his couch.

"Ruth! What are you doing here?"

"George was in the North Tower."

"Good God! I'm sorry!"

"We talked before he fell. I can't be alone tonight."

"Stay here. Let me fix you a drink."

Mike hurried out to the kitchen and mixed Ruth a strong gin and tonic. He fixed a strong one for himself.

In the living room he pulled a chair up beside the sofa. "You want to talk about it?"

"No, I just need your company. It's been a nightmare. Only it's real. And it won't stop."

"George was a fine man. This whole thing is horrible."

"There must be thousands dead. We won't know for days."

"How can I help, Ruth?"

"I'm lost, Mike. George is dead. I can't …" she started crying

Stroud moved to the couch, holding Ruth in his arms until she recovered. He fetched a pain pill from a plastic vial he had left over from being shot years earlier. Ruth swallowed it with her drink. Minutes later she became drowsy. Stroud undressed her, helping her into one of his T-shirts. He led Ruth to his king-size bed, covered her up with a sheet and blanket, and then pulled a chair over. He fixed himself another gin and tonic and sat there beside the bed the remainder of the night.

Ruth awakened once, calling George's name. Mike took her hand. Minutes later she dozed off again.

⌒

"Gran-maw, why is everybody so sad?"

"A bad thing happened, Jake. A lot of people got killed."

"Why, Gran-maw?"

"You don't need to know that. You're safe here with us."

"They won't get us?"

"No, honey. We have friends who protect us."

"Do you like Pink?"

"I love Pink. She's a wonderful singer."

"Can we see her when she comes to town?"

"Of course, dear."

"Gran-maw, why does Gran-paw go away so much?

"He has a job that takes him out of town."

"Can we go too?"

"No, baby. It's a special job that he has to do all by himself."

"Okay. I'm going out and play now."

Trudy sat at her breakfast table sipping a cup of Brazilian coffee. She knew part of what Dutch did was dangerous. He didn't tell her everything because he didn't want her to worry, and she seldom asked. She didn't want Dutch to feel obligated to explain his absences. She also knew her father had been involved with Rico and Cottonmouth in a number of secret operations. Today Dutch was in Washington. He'd told Trudy it had to do with 9/11. That concerned her, but at the same time she felt very proud of her brave husband.

⌒

General Kurtz was at his desk studying a map of India when Dutch knocked on the door. The general was expecting him. His secretary had been given the afternoon off. Kurtz didn't want anyone to overhear what they were about to discuss.

"You're looking well, general. That arm all healed up?"

"Yes, thank you. How's the family?"

"Trudy and I are blessed. The twins are both enrolled at Emory University."

"That's wonderful. We have a lead on one of those 9/11 bastards. Ruth Townsend passed this over to me last week. You know she lost her husband in the North Tower?"

"Rico told me. That's a shame. This whole thing's a rotten shame."

"As soon as I heard about that first plane I suspected bin Laden. My people think he's behind it."

"Rico said the same thing. It sounds like bin Laden to me."

"Our suspect works in the Pakistan Embassy. He's a senior courier. That's doublespeak for spy. Ruth says he's been emailing airline schedules to an Internet exchange in Afghanistan for weeks now. He also sent some maps earlier. We checked him out. He's definitely Al Qaeda.

"You got his information?"

"Got his name, work and home address, the restaurant he frequents, even where he has his dry cleaning done. He has the usual diplomatic immunity so be careful."

"I'll get with Rico on this one. It's payback time."

"We need to track them down and eliminate those sons a bitches."

"I'll see to it, general. Are you coming to Atlanta anytime soon?"

"Couple of months. Why do you ask?"

"Trudy wants to have you over for dinner. Little Jake misses you. You can stay with us."

"I'd be delighted. Your family is relaxing for me. Makes me wish I was married again. You and Trudy did a great job raising those girls."

"They're not girls anymore, general. They've blossomed into beautiful young women. I'm going to have my hands full before long."

"You'll make out. They're first class. They'd make fine Marines."

Dutch laughed. "I'll tell 'em you said so."

Dutch got up to leave. He had to beat the traffic to get to the airport on time.

"Tell Trudy hello for me. Tell Jake I'll bring him a present soon."

"I'll do it, sir. Take care of yourself."

❧

Rico was having beers with Harry, Adolfo, Eddie Nails, and Frado at the downtown marina in Miami. They were discussing the attacks in New York City. Rico was filling them in on the embassy courier. Eddie Nails had been friends with an Army major who died in the South Tower.

"George Brown was a stand-up guy. You remember him from the birthday party, don't you, Harry?"

"Right, boss. Da dude was okay."

"Ruth is heartbroken over this. That courier fuck is going down. Adolfo, I want you and Frado to handle this. Blue Pony expects you'll be delivering another package. Eddie, come up with something special this time. I want to send a message to bin Laden."

"Special like how, boss?"

"I don't know, you guys figure something out."

"I'll work on it, boss."

"Don't dey have dat special book dey read all da time?" Harry asked.

"It's called the Quran," Rico explained. "It's their bible."

Frado sat forward in his chair. "I hear they're real touchy about that bible book."

Rico smiled. "Work on it. I want bin Laden to piss his pants."

"I got a few notions." Adolfo looked thoughtful. "We'll fix that prick good."

"I'd like ta go wid youse guys."

"No, Harry, I need you here," Rico told him. "Dutch Henry is coming next week."

❧

Romadi Johiya was sitting at the front window of his favorite restaurant in Georgetown, sipping a Long Island tea. He enjoyed alcohol, all kinds of alcohol, since it was forbidden in his home country. All except that Murree Brewery leftover from colonial days. He was celebrating the Twin Towers.

A little over 2,800 died in the attacks. He wished it were 28,000, but 343 firemen and 60 policemen made him smile, plus those stupid infidels caught on the airplanes and a few more on the ground. Two big buildings, four passenger jets, and the Pentagon was a grand beginning for Islam. More would follow, much more.

Stupid Americans! Women walk around half naked. Husbands are forbidden to beat their wives. The children are spoiled monsters. All deserve the wrath of Islam. They deserve to burn in Allah's furnaces.

He dreamed of a wife like Mohammad's little Aisha, young and obedient and very pretty. She would fulfill his destiny. Make him feel like a desert warrior. Slake his sexual desires with her young body. Six and a half, maybe seven or eight, was not too young. He would teach her things, so many things. He would instruct her in the ways of the Holy Quran. And how to deceive and steal, and kill the degenerate infidels.

Dinner consisted of fresh mustard leaves stuffed with chickpeas, herbs, rice, and onions. Black pepper mutton kebab, and a savory pastry filled with herbs and goat cheese. He washed it all down with unsweetened tea then ordered a glass of Grand Cru burgundy.

Romadi enjoyed his evenings in Washington, walking along Quincy Street. It reminded him a little of home, minus the earthquakes and political unrest. Nevertheless, he much preferred Pakistan, even with her misfortunes. The infidels were blasphemers against all Arab nations. They must die—and those disgusting Jews! He prayed that Iran would get the bomb before the Americans or Israel blew up the Iranian compounds. Then Tel Aviv would burn in the nuclear fires and, soon enough, the American cities. He prayed too that Osama bin Laden was safe and well.

President Bush troubled him. That man was a cowboy, prone to violent actions against Islam. If only he could get that infidel alone, he would cut his heart out and deliver it to the mosque. What a celebration that would be. His fame would spread across the Middle East. The Great Romadi Johiya!

Entering his townhouse, Romadi sensed something was wrong. A shadow appeared before him, blowing a cloud of dust into his face. It was scopolamine, taken from the South American kidnappers when Detective McCoy was still alive. Cottonmouth had given it to Adolfo before he and Frado departed Miami. Frado had laced the drug with a heavy mixture of LSD. The effect swept over Romadi like a freight train: dizziness, palpitations of the heart, dry mouth, tunnel vision, and vivid hallucinations. Romadi felt like he was losing his mind. The enveloping darkness terrified the man. He saw the Towers burning, people falling, then the furniture began coming alive.

"I can't stand it … Allah … help me."

"We're here to help you, Mister Johiya. Stand up on the table."

"It's horrible … oh Allah … have mercy."

The carpet pulsed with spines, moving slowly across the floor. Black blood oozed down the walls.

"It's the only way we can help you."

The schefflera began reaching for Romadi … he looked down at his hands … opaque green with long black talons. The LSD was ushering him into a hallucinatory world of madness.

He whimpered in terror, climbing up on the table. "Allah … please … make it stop."

"Put that around your neck. It will keep you from falling. "

Frado had already tied the rope around an overhead beam. He got on the table beside Romadi, standing him up straight, making certain the noose was tight.

"You all set, pal?"

Romadi nodded, his face twisted in horror.

Adolfo tipped over the table. While Romadi kicked and choked, they wiped the table clean of fingerprints. It was over in a few minutes. They laid a typewritten note on the coffee table and closed the front door on their way out.

Police found the note two days later. Romadi's death was ruled a suicide.

"I can't live with myself any longer. I helped plan the 9/11 attacks. Mohammad was a false profit. Jesus Christ is the true Savior. Please forgive me.
Romadi Johiya"

A newspaper reporter with *The Washington Post* ran a photograph of the suicide note beside his news story on the front page. Protesters gathered in front of the *Post* the next morning. A thousand Muslims marched in the streets of Paris. Thirty people died in riots across the Middle East.

⸙

Moses was visiting the island where he and Karl buried their money. He went there to erect a small camouflage tent in case he had to make a fast getaway from the cabin. White Devil had killed a coyote so Moses brought that along for the reptile. Moses believed everything had a spirit: trees, mountains, birds, even the swamp. For him the swamp was a sacred place, housing millions of earth spirits. The alligator possessed an earth spirit. The coyote was dead so his earth spirit had departed to be with his spirit family. Plants and animals were earth spirits. Human beings were celestial spirits.

The trees were a mixture of males and females. Hills were female spirits. Mountains were male spirits. The wind was a gentle but sometimes angry spirit. But horses were his favorite. They represented the best of everything. He hated that the US Government was killing wild horses out west. That, for Moses, was murder.

Moses believed Karl was waiting out there in a celestial field of souls circling the earth. Human souls waited there to reunite with their loved ones before traveling on. When Moses died, he and Karl would journey to a wondrous new place where they would always enjoy peace, no more problems, no more aches and pains, sharing endless stories around eternal campfires with other warriors like themselves, males and females alike.

His cell phone rang.

"This is Mike. Are you well enough to travel?"

"Where you want to go?"

"Paris. I have a two-week vacation coming up. There's work to do there."

"Work like for us?"

"Yes."

"When we leave?"

⌇

They were sitting on a park bench beneath the Eiffel Tower where they'd been instructed to wait. Off to their left they could see the Pont d'Iéna Bridge over the Seine River. In the distance was the Place du Trocadéro. To their right were the greens and the Champ de Mars. Tourists were busy coming and going.

Blue Pony shook his head. "People like loose chickens."

A jaw-dropping redhead turned off the Musée du Quai Branly sidewalk. Men turned and stared. Women bridled. One mesmerized fellow walked into a lamppost.

"Moses, look at that."

"Hot Damn!"

As she came abreast of their small conclave of shrubs and benches, she turned to face them. Six feet tall, thirty-five years old, ample bosoms, broad shoulders, small waist, and long, well-conditioned legs. She was gorgeous with bobbed hair and wearing a fashionable black French business suit. She wore black leather slouch boots and a white silk scarf around her pretty neck, complemented by a white cloche hat.

"Gentlemen, I'm Mimi Le Beau's daughter, Rosalene. You may call me Rose. I'm your *auxiliare.*"

"Our what?"

"Your aide. I'm here to help you with your assignment."

The two men just stared.

"Come now, surely you've seen a tall lady before?"

"Tall, yes, but nothing like you."

"I get that a lot. Come with me. I have a *voiture* down the street."

"A what?"

"My automobile."

The drive south lasted a little over an hour. Rose drove her Peugeot up a long driveway to a white Victorian home atop a grassy knoll overlooking a beautiful green valley. Behind the house they observed a gray clapboard barn with a small corral. Behind the barn was a large pond. Several horses were in the field out back.

As they exited the automobile an attractive gray-haired woman appeared on the front porch.

"Ma-Ma, look what I brought you. Two handsome Americans!"

"Welcome to my home. I'm Mimi Le Beau. General Kurtz informed me you were coming. Please come inside. You must be tired from your long journey. I'll fix you a cool drink. Rose, take their bags upstairs to the front bedrooms."

"Ma'am, how do you know General Kurtz?" Mike asked.

"The general was friends with Rose's father, Master Sergeant Lucian Abernathy. He was killed before Rose was born. That's when I left Da Nang and moved here in '69. Rose was born that year. I kept in touch with some of the men who survived the war. General Kurtz told me about the things you do for your country, and about the passing of Monsieur Peters."

"I served with Dutch Henry in Vietnam, and my friend Karl Musgrove," Moses replied.

"The general paid you a great compliment, Moses. He told me you and Karl saved their lives in Tajikistan. I'm sorry your friend was killed."

"Karl was brave man."

Mike studied the woman. "The general must place great stock in you to tell you these things."

"Robert and I used to discuss politics when he was still a colonel. That was before the Tet Offensive when I ran my little business in Da Nang. We believed then that the world was headed for trouble. Years later he met Ruth Townsend at Monsieur Peters' home in Atlanta. That's when he decided to join our group. Robert told me Ruth's husband, George, was killed in those 9/11 attacks. I've never met Ruth, but she sounds like a courageous woman."

"She's the best. I hope to marry that girl someday."

"That may come to pass sooner than you think, Michael."

"Tell them, Ma-Ma."

"Rose is the impetuous type. She gets that from her father."

"Tell us what, Mrs. Le Beau."

"The general and I planned this operation. Lydia Sams was notified, so London is on standby in case we need their help. Rose has agreed to play the role of decoy, so I believe the four of us can pull it off."

"Ma-Ma paints the pretty picture, no? There's going to be an attempt to collapse the French franc."

"Who would do this thing?" Moses asked.

"Boris Sokolov is a money manipulator. The Bilderbergs are involved, and possibly a few of your politicians. For them it's the money, always it's the money—and political control."

"Our politicians, are you serious?"

"The trail went cold in San Diego. We believe someone in California is part of the plot."

"That is disgusting."

"Boris Sokolov got the idea from George Soros. Soros has bought and sold politicians all over the world. Their ultimate goal, you see, is globalization with the superrich from those secret societies controlling a centralized government."

"But how could they damage the French monetary system?" Mike asked.

Rose explained. "The French economy is unstable. It has been for some time because of our liberal politicians and the European Union. Sokolov and his billionaire friends are going to short sell the franc then buy them back when the market falls. To promote the decline, they have a banker in Paris ready to flood the market with counterfeit notes. German Intelligence intercepted this information seven weeks ago then alerted General Kurtz. The general consulted his Foreign Legion friends in Aubagne. The Deutsche Bundesbank was notified. Germany's central banking committee has agreed to head off the crisis."

"Robert worked with the German BND for years," Mimi said. "They know what Soros did in Russia and those Eastern Bloc countries. The Bundesnachrichtendienst knows the bank, and they know the date of the sale. Germany is going to back the franc as soon as Sokolov makes his move. The franc will go up, and Sokolov and his gang of conspirators will lose a fortune."

"Ma-Ma and I are going to intercept the money. The general assigned that job to us. I'll pretend motor trouble on the side of the road while wearing my old miniskirt. It's quite daring. When the driver stops, Moses and I will commandeer the truck. If he drives on, Ma-Ma and Michael will be waiting over the hill with our farm truck blocking the bridge."

"How much is road used?" Moses asked.

"It's an old Roman roadway used mostly by the farmers," Mimi replied.

"When's that sale going down?"

Rose smiled. "Eight days from today. The truck is supposed to deliver the francs the next morning. The bank is going to flood the market two weeks after that. It's an Afghan bank used for money laundering.

"Our Legion will take those men into custody the day the truck is scheduled to arrive. They have a man who can imitate the banker's voice. If Sokolov calls to verify delivery, he will be none the wiser."

"What we do with funny money?"

"The Legion Commandant gave us his blessing. He wants this business kept quiet and the money destroyed. Parisian authorities will not be informed, too many loose tongues in that administration. The Marne River isn't far from the old highway. Ma-Ma and I picked a secluded spot. We'll drive the truck there then run it off a cliff. The river is very deep there."

"What about driver?"

"A Legionnaire will be with Ma-Ma and Michael. He will arrest the driver. "

Three days passed with the women showing the men around the farm on horseback. It took Mike a bit of getting used to, learning to ride his Camargue mare. Blue Pony was a natural, having ridden horses as a boy. French cooking and the country air proved a tonic for both men. It was a nice escape from the rigors of life back in America.

Moses was almost asleep when he heard his bedroom door open and close. Rosalene was coming across the room in the moonlight. She sat down on the edge of his bed.

"We have problem?"

"Everything is fine. I want to ask you something."

"Okay, I listen."

"Six years ago my husband was killed in Algiers. He was a lieutenant with the French Foreign Legion. We had planned on children, but Peter died before that happened. Since then I've searched for a suitable partner, but real men are hard to find in today's politically correct world. When I saw you on that bench, I thought, yes, maybe he's the one. These past three days have been wonderful. I admire you very much, Monsieur Blue Pony. I want you to give me a baby."

"You mean… You mean now?"

"Yes, Moses, make me pregnant."

"Mike will hear."

"The walls are thick. Mike will hear nothing."

"What about Mama?"

"Ma-Ma and I discussed a child. She thinks it's a marvelous idea."

Moses reached for the little pink bow on the front of Rosalene's nightgown. The nightie slid down, revealing her voluptuous breasts. She stood, letting the nightgown fall away. In the moonlight she appeared radiant, almost like an angel.

La deésse de la beauté and her champion.

Rose lay back. When he kissed her, she parted her legs, guiding the handsome Cherokee into her warm and delicious body. Their romantic interludes lasted four exotic nocturnes.

⌣

Rosalene was bent over her Peugeot, the hood up, her short miniskirt revealing her attractive bottom to the oncoming truck laden with the counterfeit bank notes. The truck slowed to a halt. Moses lay hidden behind a stand of bushes just off the road.

"Moses! Help Me! "

Blue Pony emerged from his hiding place to find two men holding Rose on the ground. They had punched her nearly senseless. The big one was holding her down while the smaller man pulled her panties off. He began unbuttoning his trousers with a malicious grin on his face.

"Paleface having good time?"

The short man sprang to his feet, pulling a switchblade from his pants pocket. Blue Pony shot him between the eyes. The big one pulled a revolver. Moses shot him before he could bring his gun to bear.

Moses knelt down beside Rose, wiping the blood away from her nose.

She shielded her eyes against the sun, gazing up at him. "Those men … you killed them ..."

"Men needed killing."

"I think you just saved my life."

"You okay now. You rest awhile."

"Moses, I want to ask you something."

"Woman full of questions."

"You like me, don't you?"

"I like you very much, Rosie."

"Will you stay with me?"

"You serious?"

"I don't want you to go away, ever."

"I'm nearly fifty-one, you still a young woman."

"That doesn't matter to me."

"Knock on head make you crazy."

"No, dear, I want you to be the Pa-Pa of our children."

"I'm worn-out old Injun man."

"You certainly weren't worn out last night, or those other nights!"

"I disappoint you?"

"No, *mon chéri*. You're *mon bebe*."

"I'm glad you think so."

"Underneath that bark and bite, you're a gallant man."

"Karl would say sure, okay, yes."

"Please stay, Moses."

"Many moons I dream of woman like you."

"I'm yours if you want me."

"You make me proud, Rosie. What Mama say?"

"Ma-Ma wants you to stay too."

"I stay then. You want get married?"

"Oh yes, Moses. Yes! I want very much to be your *compagne*."

"When this is over, we quit dangerous business."

"*Oui, mon cheri*, for the sake of our little ones."

"I ask Lone Ranger first."

"Who?"

"Bad joke, Rosie. Is great honor to be your man, but first I go home for my animals. I have money to bring back."

"What kind of animals?"

"Two dogs an' one ole cat."

"Our doggie died. Ma-Ma will adore your *animaux de compagnie*."

Mike, Mimi, and a Legion colonel pulled up just as Blue Pony was loading the last body into the back of the Citroen van.

"Ma-Ma, he's going to stay!"

Chapter Nineteen

Iraq

Saddam Hussein was a ruthless and brutal dictator. For years he ruled Iraq with an iron fist, torturing and murdering tens of thousands of his own countrymen. Uday, his eldest son, evolved from a spoiled Sunni brat into a flamboyant psychopathic sex-crazed monster. He was noted for picking out the prettiest schoolgirls, having them forcibly delivered to his palace, raping them for days, and sometimes killing them or having them murdered by his palace guards. Qusay, his younger brother by two years, was another Sunni killer who lived in the shadow of Uday and his evil father, Saddam. They terrorized Iraq until Iraqi Freedom rolled into town March 20, 2003.

Nigger and White Trash had gotten themselves separated from their squad.

They'd just opened the door to a torture chamber beneath one of Saddam's opulent palaces. Trash, Antonio Lomascolo, was a twenty-three year old Italian American from Poughkeepsie, New York. Nigger,

Marcus Johnson, was a twenty-four year old African American from El Dorado, Arkansas. The two had gotten into a fistfight at Parris Island during boot camp. They fought until they were both exhausted. Afterward, they became best friends. The names they called one another stuck.

"Hey, Trash, check this out."

"What is it?"

"It's where they hung people up an' whooped 'em."

"From them hooks up there, looks like."

"Yeah. Hung 'em up like sides uh beef then whooped their asses."

"There's the stuff they used."

Trash was pointing to an assortment of whips and knotted ropes hanging from pegs on a support column. Beneath the whips sat a wooden table laden with tools, knives, clubs, and a Black & Decker power drill.

"What's that thing?

"Looks like somethin' they stuck their legs in."

"Jesus! It's got teeth in it."

The device had a metal crank with a wooden handle. It was a steel case attached to a wooden chair anchored to the concrete floor. The device was used for torture and extracting information. Four other chairs sat along the back wall with plastic restraints for securing a victim's wrists and ankles. A stainless steel table with rubber tethers sat in the middle of the bare-bulb atmosphere. There were blood stains on the floor and around the walls.

"I hope they catch that sumbitch an' string 'im up by 'is pecker!"

"Nigger, if we get trapped someplace an' I'm shot up bad, don't let 'em get me. You know what they do to Marines. Just shoot my ass and be done with it."

"Don't worry, bro. You'll do the same thing for me, okay?"

"I'll do it, Nig. I won't let those bastards get their hands on ya."

"Right on. Let's get the hell outta this stink hole."

A loud explosion knocked both men back inside the room, flat on their backs. The wooden door was blown to pieces. Trash had a large sliver of wood embedded through the top of his left boot. Nigger had splinters in his chest and shoulder.

"Get this thing outta me."

"Hang on a minute. I'm stuck too."

Nigger retrieved a pair of pliers from the table and pulled out his splinters. Then he set about removing a footlong splinter from Antonio's leg.

"That thing's in there an inch or two."

"Just pull it out, damn it. We got company!"

Nigger pulled the bloody piece of wood from his friend's leg then took a quick look around the door frame. Shots rang out.

"How many grenades you got?"

"Two frags. You?"

"One frag and one smoke. I bet them assholes worked in here. I'm gonna send 'em a little present."

Nigger popped the handle on a fragmentation grenade then hurled it down the hallway. Then he popped a second handle and flung that one. Two explosions … howls of pain. Marcus rushed out the door.

Blam! Blam! Blam! Blam! Blam!

"I sent three of 'em up to see ole Allah. One raghead got out the back. You okay, Trash?"

"You're killer, man. You got more balls than a go-rilla."

"Can you walk?"

"I believe so. Let's find the squad."

Two doors down the hallway, Trash whispered for his friend to stop. "You hear that? Sounds like a woman crying."

"Stand back. I'll shoot the lock."

Blam!

"Holy Dog Shit!"

Inside, the Marines found four women, buck naked. Two beds, a table with dirty dishes, and six wooden chairs sat on a trash-littered floor.

"Damn, ladies, ain't cha got no clothes?"

"They burn our clothes. Uday rape us. Guards rape us."

"Where'd they go?"

"They leave this morning."

"How many?"

"Ten, maybe."

"Trash, we gotta get these girls somethin' to wear."

"I'll see what I can round up."

"You ladies want anything?"

"Water, please. We have nothing to drink for long time."

"Stay here, I'll find ya something."

Nigger went down the hallway. One of the torturers was still alive. He shot the man again. There were five one-gallon jugs of water sitting beside the backdoor. Marcus confiscated a jug.

Trash found Iraqi uniforms, but no female attire.

The women put on the shirts with their pretty bottoms showing. The pants were too big and too long.

"They need some underwear and some shoes."

Trash left again, returning with military skivvies and cotton socks. "That's it, hoss. They ain't nothin' else down here."

"Ladies, put these on. You'll catch a cold with yer fannies hangin' out."

The girls giggled.

The two Marines led them out of the palace into an elegant court-yard. Outside, they found their squad bivouacked a quarter mile down the road.

"Whoa! Whaddaya got there? Looks like hootenanny time."

Trash turned on the speaker. "Shut up your face or I'll bust you one."

"That goes double for me, you dumb cracker!"

"Damn, fellas," the Marine said. "I didn't mean nothin' by it."

"These ladies been through hell, got that?"

"Gotcha, Nig. I'm sorry, ladies."

"You guys got any canned peaches or pears?" Trash asked. "They're hungry."

The Marines gathered around, sharing fruit and candy bars with the teenagers. A sand-colored Humvee pulled up.

Major Pyle stepped out. "What the hell is this?"

"Me an' Trash here rescued these ladies from that palace up yonder. They been treated pretty bad, major."

"What's your name, Marine?"

"Sergeant Marcus Johnson, sir."

"Who's your sidekick there?

"Corporal Antonio Lomascolo, sir."

"That's a mouthful. You men got anything to report?"

"Nigger here, I mean Sergeant Johnson, killed three uh the enemy, sir."

"Saddam's son, Uday, and about ten guards left here this morning, major."

"Where'd you get that information?"

"These ladies told us, sir."

"Good job, fellas! I'll report this to HQ. I got some brass to meet so I better get a move on. I'll call for a helicopter to pick up these girls. You two go with them. Get those wounds tended to. You Marines be careful out there, *comprende*?"

"Yes Sir!"

〜

They were recuperating in an air-conditioned hospital room in Karbala, 75 miles SW of Baghdad.

"How's the leg?"

"I'm cool, man. You?"

"I got little bandages stuck all over. These pain pills are great, man."

"Yeah, it hurt 'til they gave me some."

"Those girls were pretty, weren't they?"

"Yeah. Naked as jaybirds. Folks back home won't believe us."

"You goin' back to bein' a mechanic when you get out?"

"I been thinkin', Trash. I know engines. And you sold automotive parts. Wanna try a business of our own back in the world?"

"Heck, Yeah! We'd make a killer team."

"We could go to Birmingham, Atlanta, Orlando, lots uh places where we could start a business."

"What about Atlanta? They got four or five million people there."

"That's my favorite too."

"Okay, let's set our sights on Atlanta."

"We could open a parts store, buy old cars, and fix 'em up. People pay good money for a good used car."

"We'll need a business license," Trash reminded him.

"I know a man in Atlanta that can help us. He was friends with my daddy in Vietnam. He came to the house a couple uh times before Daddy died."

"I'm sorry your daddy passed away."

"They buried Pop in Arlington. His heart gave out when I was fourteen."

"What's the man's name?"

"Dutch Henry. He's an older gentleman. A bunch uh those guys used to get together ever' year to party an' talk about the war. They always had an empty chair at the end of the table for their dead buddies."

"You know, Nig, I never thought much about this war business 'til we got over here. Politicians are good at gambling with other people's lives. We coulda gotten our asses killed back there by that RPG. I wonder if this shit is worth all the trouble."

"Daddy talked about Vietnam sometimes. He called Johnson a dumb son of a bitch. Said the man was a control freak. Said he didn't know squat about winning a war. He said we coulda won the Vietnam War if Johnson had kept his nose out of it."

"That's for sure."

"Why didn't we finish the first Gulf War, Trash? That way we wouldn't be here in this hospital. I don't get politicians."

"My father told me something when I was a sophomore in high school. He said don't believe what you read in the newspapers, and don't trust the politicians."

"Sounds like your daddy's a pretty smart feller."

"Funny how we take our parents for granted when we're young and stupid. Then later on the things they told us start to sink it."

"Amen, brother. I didn't have my head screwed on 'til I got in the Corps."

"I never told anybody this before, but I want you to know, Nig. My father grew up in an Italian neighborhood. Some uh those guys joined the Mob. Over the years they told him things. Part of it I know is true. Some of it sounds pretty nuts."

"Your father was in the Mafia?"

"No, but he knows some of them. They told him that during the 1930s the Dulles and the Bush families helped finance Hitler. It was all about money. Everything was about money. LBJ was a crook, and the big boys in Texas knew it. The Chicago Mob helped swing the election for Kennedy against Nixon. Then Bobby Kennedy betrayed the Mob, an' started puttin' 'em in jail."

"I didn't know that."

"That ain't all. Back then the CIA was killing people all over the world, especially South America and over here in the Middle East. When the Kennedys turned on the Mob and JFK started havin' second thoughts about Vietnam, the Mob guys and the CIA set up three different locations to kill the president. Number one was Tampa, Florida. I forgot the second one. The third was Dallas, Texas.

"Oswald was a paid FBI informer. He was the fall guy in Dallas.

That policeman that got killed in Dallas was supposed to kill Oswald. He blew it so the CIA killed him then dropped a fake Oswald wallet at the crime scene. The cops arrested Oswald so Jack Ruby was assigned to kill him. It's believed those same people killed Bobby Kennedy and Martin Luther King.

"The Warren Commission lied about the whole damn thing.

"Johnson knew about those South American murders. He knew the Kennedys were thinking about exposing his criminal ass in Texas too. LBJ made millions off his crooked deals and the Vietnam War. Pop said after Kennedy was killed, the CIA murdered some witnesses. Pop thinks most politicians are dumb as dirt. The rest are in on those crooked deals."

"Sounds like we're bein' run by crooks an' dumbasses."

"We have been ever since the Great Depression. Keep quiet about what I just told you. I don't want somebody going after my pop someday."

"You have my word, Trash. When we get home we'll have to stop using our nicknames. All that political correctness stuff, ya know."

"I gotcha. From now on I'm calling you Asshole!"

"Say what?"

"Just kidding. I'm gonna start calling you Marcus so I can get used to it.

"Cool, man. From now on I'll call you Tony."

Uday and Qusay Hussein were killed in a three-hour firefight by Allied Forces inside the town of Mosul on July 22, 2003. Saddam Hussein was captured hiding in spider hole in Tikrit on December 13, 2003. Allied Forces were instructed to fight a politically correct war. It was a Vietnam police action all over again, with the Rules of Engagement being written by lawyers and politicians in air-conditioned boardrooms. Fighting would drag on for years with Abu Musab al-Zarqawi and his Muslim lieutenants leading the Islamic insurgency against the Allies.

Marcus and Antonio signed on for a second tour of duty on March 5, 2004.

Two months after returning to the field they walked into an ambush in a suburb outside Fallujah. Second Squad was pinned down in a drainage ditch in front of a mosque where machine gun and automatic rifle fire was pouring out the front windows. Two Marines were hit immediately. Tony and Marcus ran behind a mud-brick wall a few yards left of the ditch. Sergeant Marcus radioed an Abrams battle tank for assistance. A few minutes later the tank rolled up beside the wall. Bullets rang off her steel turret.

"The Rules of Engagement says we ain't supposed to fire on a mosque."

"Fuck the Rules of Engagement. Them assholes shot two of my men."

"That's different, I reckon. Are you sure about this, sergeant?"

"I'll take full responsibility. Blow those sonsabitches away."

The gunner loaded a high explosive shell into his breech and pulled the trigger. The front door and part of the front wall exploded in a cloud of smoke and flame. He loaded another HE round and fired again. The left side of the building sagged then collapsed. Eight combatants came running out the front, screaming, "Allah Akbar, Allah Akbar." A third Marine caught a 7.62mm round through his arm. The gunner rammed a 120mm grapeshot canister into his breech.

BOOM!

Tungsten balls, about 1,150 of them, blew the eight running men to shreds.

"Those bastards had to be hopped up on something," Tony remarked.

"Well, they ain't hopped up no more. Let's see about our wounded."

Two weeks later Marcus and Tony were standing in the chow line at a mess hall in Baghdad. A major and a captain walked up with two MPs.

"Is your name Johnson, Sergeant Marcus Johnson?"

"Yes, sir."

"You'll have to come with us, Johnson. You're under arrest."

"What's he charged with, sir?"

"What's your name?"

"Corporal Antonio Lomascolo, sir."

"You're the other one we're looking for."

"On what charge, sir?"

"You blew up a mosque and killed eleven civilians."

"Civilians, my ass. They shot three of our men!"

"Belay that! You're coming with us!"

⸗

The military tribunal had been in session an hour. Army Captain Rufus King, who assisted with the arrest, was chief council for the prosecution. A Marine first lieutenant, James Buchanan, had been assigned to defend the two Marines charged with violating the ROE. Buchanan was a law school graduate from the University of Alabama. Barrister Buchanan was a soft-spoken Southern gentleman. He held a faint resemblance to Leslie Howard.

Three Iraqi residents living near the mosque had been subpoenaed by the prosecution. All three swore that Johnson and Lomascolo were responsible for destroying the mosque, and the deaths of the fourteen civilians.

Believing he had a slam dunk, Captain King was grilling the three Marines who had been wounded in the firefight. Captain King was an imposing figure, 6'2", 195 pounds, with dusty yellow hair and piercing brown eyes. He'd graduated in the top of his class from Harvard Law School.

"And isn't it true, gentlemen, that you would say or do just about anything to save your Marine buddies from spending time in Leavenworth?"

"No, Nigger an'… I mean Johnson and the corporal are good men. They saved our butts out there."

"Nigger? Why do you refer to your African American sergeant as Nigger?"

"Well it's just a nickname, sir. Him 'n' Trash got in a fight at Parris Island an' …"

"Trash?"

"You see, sir, they got in this fistfight when they …"

"Got into a fistfight? Were they fighting the day they blew up the mosque?"

"No, sir. That mosque was full of ragheads. They were shooting at us."

"Ragheads! I believe that explains the whole story behind this squad of killers. Marines are notorious for cruelty to civilians as well as combatants. That was the case in the Pacific and the Korean War."

"Objection!" Lieutenant Buchanan stood. "The prosecution is not an expert on Marines or their table manners."

"Objection overruled!"

A full-bird pear-shaped colonel was the presiding judge. He held the gavel. He'd been passed over twice for promotion to brigadier due to his political affiliations. He was a belligerent man who disliked the military, President Bush, and especially Marines. He was arrogant and dismissive of military ranks below his own.

A second Marine was summoned to testify.

Lieutenant Buchanan opened. "Son, tell the tribunal what you saw out there the day in question."

"Well, sir, I was down in this ditch an' bullets were flying all over. I couldn't see much because of all the smoke, but Sergeant Johnson an' Trash … I mean …"

King interrupted. "There it is again, Johnson and Trash. These two weren't friends. They were out to prove to their squad mates who the best man was. The toughest Marine. They murdered those innocent civilians."

"Objection! That is biased opinion on the part of the prosecution."

"Objection overruled!"

Buchanan tried again. "There was gunfire coming from the mosque the day in question. Is that correct?"

"Objection! Council is leading the witness."

"Sustained!"

The charade of injustice went on for another two hours. Finally, the colonel called a recess for lunch. It was apparent Marcus and Tony were being railroaded by a prejudicial tribunal.

"Looks like our goose is cooked, Lieutenant." Marcus was despondent.

"I can file an appeal. What those officers are doing is criminal."

"This is crazy. We were doing our jobs out there, trying to save our guys."

"I believe you, Tony. I'll do my best to take this to a higher court."

Tony and Marcus were too depressed to eat. They sipped Coca-Colas and waited. The tribunal was reconvened at one o'clock. The colonel pounded his gavel, and the courtroom came to order.

Their guilt was a foregone conclusion. Captain King began his summation.

The doors opened and three officers walked in, followed by four MPs. It was the tank commander, Major Pyle, and Marine Lieutenant General Buford McMahan. A stir went through the room.

The colonel pounded his gavel for silence. "What are you doing in my courtroom?"

General McMahan glared at the colonel. "Your courtroom, my ass! Stand at attention when I'm addressing you!"

The colonel turned beet red and stood up.

"You, there, Captain King. You ever been in a firefight?

"Well, uh … Well, no, sir … I'm … I'm a military lawyer."

"You got that half right, King. You're a lawyer. There's nothing military about you or this buffoon of a colonel or any of you Star Chamber yardbirds. This lieutenant and his defendants are the only military present, besides me and my boys, here. "

King spoke up. "Sir, I object to that remark.

"Did you investigate the crime scene, captain?"

"Well, uh, no … We … We have these three witnesses who testified."

"There are hundreds of cartridge casings inside that mosque. We went in and looked. You're a disgrace to the uniform, King!"

"Well, uh, you see, sir—"

"Shut up and sit down!"

The colonel found his voice. "Sir, I object."

"Shut your pie hole, colonel. Speak only when you're spoken to. Tell 'em, Johnny."

The tank commander stepped to the front of the room. He still wore his battle fatigues and a sidearm. The man was sweat-stained and dirty.

"When Major Pyle radioed me I was 100 miles northeast uh here. It took me all morning to get back. I radioed the general on my way in. These two Marines were dead on when they asked me to fire on that mosque. It was full of insurgents. A bunch of 'em come runnin' out the front door firing AK-47s. My gunner blew 'em away. I reckon those others were killed inside the building. We saw three go out the back way. I 'spect that's them right there, general."

"Boys, arrest those lying bastards! And you sonsabitches are going on report. I'll have your asses sacked from my Armed Forces. Go back to Washington where clusterfucks like you live and breed."

"This is an outrage. You have no right!" the colonel blustered.

"And throw his fat ass in the brig for insubordination, abuse of the military code, prosecutorial misconduct, and bein' a dickhead! Come with me, Marines. This trial is over!"

Chapter Twenty

Peter Engel

Following an extended period of sadness and a puddle of tears, Ruth Townsend had finally accepted her husband's death in the 9/11 attacks. Mike Stroud was preparing a steak dinner. They were on the back porch at his place where Mike was officiating over a charcoal grill.

"I have an Army buddy who worked at the Pentagon after he got back from Vietnam. Dan told me he would go home after work and take long, hot showers because he felt dirty working with those people."

"I understand, Mike. It's no different with a lot of CIA officials and politicians. They all have their agendas. Many of them are hard-core liberals."

"I don't get it. What do they see in that stuff?"

"I believe it has to do with their perception of reality. Look at Hollywood. Those pampered fools come out with things like, 'America is evil,' and 'We're responsible for all the troubles in the world.' The media is just as complicit, and just as ignorant."

"What have we done to promote slavery or people getting their heads chopped off? When we won World War II, many of those countries were set free for the first time in their history."

"It doesn't matter. To the Liberal mindset it's our fault. Logic has no effect on those people."

"Something else I don't get is this Homeland Security business. That's just another Washington bureaucracy with miles of red tape and political deadwood."

"When President Bush got elected, the people thought he was a big conservative. Bush was a RINO from the get-go, Republican in Name Only. The national debt increased 100% during his eight years in office. That's not conservative leadership, Mike."

"I guess I'm naïve. I keep hoping for another Reagan."

"Democrats will tell anyone who listens, that Trickledown Economics doesn't work. They point out that Reagan's budgets ran in the red. But that's because when all that money started pouring into the Treasury, Democrats and Republicans alike went crazy with their spending bills. Trickle Down works just fine so long as taxes are kept under control, and the politicians don't spend all the money."

"It makes no sense. Seems to me they'd want people to have more money."

"The Left wants one thing, Mike. Control! They don't give a damn about capitalism or the military or the people or you and me. They want a one-party system with them running the show."

"It didn't used to be that way. I remember when Tip O'Neal and President Reagan got along pretty well."

"That's before Lyndon Johnson and his Great Society. He and McNamara started the Vietnam War all by themselves. McGeorge Bundy, Dean Rusk, and a handful of Johnson insiders were contemplating an American defeat as early as 1964. But they kept the war going to save political face. They have blood on their hands, the same as LBJ and McNamara. And the Joint Chiefs didn't have the balls to step up to the plate and say, 'Enough.' Those silly civilians were as clueless about Vietnam as JFK was about Cuba. Nixon was starting to pull our chestnuts out of the fire when he got stuck with Watergate. The president was forced to resign, Congress cut off aid to South Vietnam in '74 and '75, and Hanoi won the war."

"I'm beginning to dislike politicians. You want yours rare or medium?"

"Make mine a skosh over medium, please."

"For you, Ruth, I'd sit on the grill myself."

"Okay, put it on there, mister."

"Hey, wait a minute. I was just kidding."

"Oh no you don't. I'm going to grill your butt, Michael Stroud."

Ruth approached Mike, pretending she was going to push him back on the hot grill. Instead, she placed her arms around his neck and kissed him. It was a long and tender kiss.

"I've wanted to do that for some time, Mike, but I had to be sure I was ready."

"Are you ready, Ruth?"

"Yes, Michael. I am."

He took her in his arms and peeled off her clothing. Then he laid Ruth down on his divan and they made love. It was their first time since high school graduation in the backseat of his old jalopy. Afterward they lay there, holding one another.

Ruth sighed. "I'd forgotten how nice it was with you."

"Did I pass muster?"

"I'm not sure. Think you can manage again?"

Their second union lasted much longer. Ruth lay back with a smile on her face, fully content. Mike laid his head on her chest and closed his eyes.

"I think you'll do just fine, Mister Stroud."

"I want you to be my wife, Ruth."

"I accept your proposal, sir."

Mike helped her up and they sat together on the divan. Michael grew misty eyed.

"I've thought about you ever since high school. Work got in the way. You went your way and I went mine. You married George. I'm sorry he got killed. Now here we are again. We've come full circle, Ruth."

"You were my hero in high school. Then we took our separate paths. I did love George, but that's behind me now. I want to be your wife, Michael. I want to make you happy."

Mike held her and kissed her again. Ruth laid her head on his shoulder.

"Our steaks are going to burn," she warned.

"I'll put 'em back in the freezer. Let's go to Freddy's tonight. I want us to celebrate."

"Yes, darling. You're still my hero."

The year 2005 was a festive year. Johnny Depp and Julia Roberts won the People's Choice Awards for motion pictures. George W. Bush began his second term as President. Condoleezza Rice was sworn in as U.S. Secretary of State. Israel and the Palestinians agreed on a ceasefire. Ice Cube won a portion of the nineteenth Soul Train Music Awards. Cardinal Joseph Ratzinger was elected Pope Benedict XVI. Syria completed its withdrawal from Lebanon, ending 29 years of occupation. Kuwait finally permitted women's suffrage. And Mark Felt revealed himself to be the anonymous Deep Throat during the Watergate investigations.

Terrorist bomb blasts struck London's public transit system, killing 52 and injuring 700. Three bombs exploded in the Naama Bay area of Sharm el-Sheikh, Egypt, killing 88 people. The first-ever joint military exercise took place between China and Russia. Then Hurricane Katrina slammed into the Gulf Coast, killing an estimated 1,839 and causing more than 115 billion dollars in damages.

The first presidential election was held in Egypt. Controversial drawings of Mohammad were printed in a Danish newspaper. Muslim riots and killings followed around the globe. The Kashmir earthquake struck parts of southern Asia. Saddam Hussein went on trial in Baghdad for crimes against humanity. Suicide bombers attacked three hotels in Amman, Jordan, killing 60 people and wounding scores of others. Tens of thousands of Hong Kong residents marched in the city streets demanding democracy. The F-22 Raptor was introduced into the USAF. And an immigration judge ordered John Demjanjuk to be deported to the Ukraine for war crimes committed during World War II.

Meanwhile, thousands of innocent civilians were tortured and murdered by Islamic fundamentalists across Africa and the Middle East.

⌒

But all was not copacetic in the Land of Smoke and Mirrors and political doublespeak.

Fannie Mae and Freddie Mac were drifting along peacefully in their fantasy world of Washington politics. "Happy days are here again," sang John Kerry and Edward Moore Kennedy. There was nary a thought on the part of the DNC and her crew as to what might lie around yonder bend.

Hark! Are those cascading rapids one hears up ahead?

The Bush Administration requested stricter regulations seventeen times to try and safeguard the government-backed secondary mortgage market. John McCain sponsored a bill attempting to head off what Republicans perceived as a gathering financial storm with subprime mortgages.

Between 2005 and 2007 subprime mortgages totaled one trillion dollars in toxic assets. The banks bundled those mortgages, selling them to Fannie and Freddie and unsuspecting investors. An avalanche of foreclosures soon followed.

Requests for caution were rejected again and again. Harry Reid and Nancy Pelosi were instrumental in defeating the McCain bill. Had it been passed by Congress, the whole controversy might have been avoided. Hundreds of thousands of loans were made to borrowers with bad credit and, in some instances, no credit at all. But that was the politically correct thing to do according to Congressional Democrats.

John McCain and the Republicans did not follow through with their efforts to head off the crisis. That was a tragic political blunder on the part of the GOP.

Barney Frank, ranking Democrat on the House Financial Services Committee, was engaged in a homosexual relationship with Herb Moses. Barney got Herb his job with Fannie Mae in 1991. Moses was awarded an influential position with the financial institution. Congressman Frank threatened the banking industry with government retaliation if they refused to make subprime loans. After all, Fannie Mae and Freddie Mac stood behind those mortgages. So the banks jumped in the deep end of the pool. Millions in commissions were made. In 1998 Barney and Herb split the blanket. Moses left the failing agency soon thereafter.

Leading up to the financial meltdown, Maxine Waters, House Representative from California, assured America that nothing was wrong at Fannie and Freddie. Waters was nowhere near qualified to render a financial opinion, and neither were most politicians on Capitol Hill.

Meanwhile Christopher Dodd, Senate Banking Committee Chairman, was preparing to run for president in 2006, so his mind was off wandering among the nether regions of political fame and glory. Dodd was awarded below-market interest rates on his Washington and Connecticut homes. And Fannie and Freddie both contributed to his political campaigns. Dodd always maintained there was nothing wrong with the two financial institutions.

Frank Raines, Chief Executive Officer for Fannie and Freddie, stepped down in 2004 when a regulator accused the agency of manipulating reports. It was believed by many that Raines knew of and contributed to the financial calamity, but that was never proven in a court of law.

A community organizer by the name of Barack Obama played a minor role in the financial fiasco. He, accompanied by ACORN and the SEIU, supported subprime mortgages while signing up minorities to vote. That expanded the Democratic voting base throughout Illinois.

⌐

"Boo, I heard a song this morning that blew me knickers off."

"What was it, babe?"

"'Learning to Fly' by Pink Floyd."

"Can you hum a few bars?"

"You silly goose!"

"Seriously, how does it go?"

"You promise you won't poke fun?"

"I promise, honor bright."

"Well, it's a little hard to describe but I think it goes like this. It's about a misfit, a dreamer, gazing up at the sky, imagining an escape from his earthbound world. Then he discovers he can fly."

"That sounds like a prisoner."

"I thought it described us."

"You're no misfit, but I think I know what you're driving at."

"Okay, tell me."

"We're learning to fly, you and me."

"You are a quick study, Mister Smarty Britches."

"I have a good professor. You!"

All morning long Lydia had put off telling Uriah the latest report from Ruth Townsend in Virginia. It was indeed bad news, both for Israel and the West.

"Ruth Townsend called. We have a problem."

"What is it?"

"North Korea. They're about to ship a bomb."

"Ship a bomb? What kind of bomb?"

"It's an atomic bomb. The CIA has a spy inside the North Korean nuclear facilities. It's going out in two weeks aboard a cargo ship headed for Iran, the *Kang Nam 8*. The ship has been fitted with lead shielding to hide its cargo signature from satellite surveillance. But we know the ship and we know the course it'll be taking."

"My God, Lydia! If Iran gets hold of that thing, you know what they'll do with it."

"I know. That's why I waited 'til after eggy toast to tell you."

"If we inform Tel Aviv they'll want to know our source. We can't do that."

"Ruth told me to keep it a secret. She asked us to coordinate with General Kurtz and Dutch Henry. They'll know what to do."

∽

"That's it, Dutch. We got two weeks to get our shit together. Sri Lanka looks like the obvious choice. Lydia Sams has all the funds we'll need. You got any suggestions?"

"If we use aircraft they'll be picked up on radar. They can't fly low enough to evade a ship's detection devices, and we don't need that hassle. What about a small warship? It could be in and out in a matter of hours."

"Blacks Ops should have something. I'll check with my Marine buddy."

"Good luck, general."

"I'll call you back tonight."

∽

"We hit this one outta the ballpark, Dutch. Peter says they got PT boats and a Fletcher-class destroyer. They got all kinds of aircraft left over from Air America. Hell, they even have a German U-boat."

"How reliable is this guy, general?"

"We soldiered together in 'Nam. They don't come any better."

"I suppose we should tell him what's onboard."

"That's not a problem. Peter wouldn't care anyway."

"What do you think our options are?"

"I like the idea of a destroyer. But that would take over a hundred men, and a boat that size has too much radar presence. Those PT boats, they're fast and their signatures are as small as tits on a mouse."

"Two should do the trick. And some kind of backup in case there's a storm or mechanical problems. We have to sink that boat, general."

"I'll have a couple of B-25s on standby."

"That'll work."

"Peter says we have a safe harbor in Sri Lanka. You interested in taking a trip with me?"

"I hadn't thought about it, but why not?"

"Get your gear together. Meet me here Wednesday, say 1400 hours."

"I'll be here, my friend."

⁓

Peter Engel was a thin, almost emaciated individual with a thick crop of blond hair and a handlebar mustache. He was 5'11", with piercing blue eyes, and the fluid movement of a cat. Sporting a green Marine T-shirt, he had a tattoo on his left arm of a Black Ops skull, wearing the traditional black beret. On his right arm was the Marine Corps globe and anchor. Peter was fifty-five years old and slowly dying from Agent Orange. He was a veteran of two wars and three secret campaigns.

"Damn, Peter. You lost more weight."

"It comes with the territory, general. I got a few years left in me."

"I want you to meet a good friend of mine, Dutch Henry."

Peter and Dutch shook hands.

"It's my good fortune, Dutch. I needed an excuse to get away from the office."

"Peter and I were stationed at Quang Tri during the Easter Offensive. That was another Intelligence fuckup. Our ARVN battalion got shot all to blazes."

"I heard about that," Dutch said. "My outfit shipped stateside a few years earlier."

"Come on down, gentlemen," Peter invited. "Let's see what's behind curtain number one."

They descended a pathway of stone steps laid into the hillside down to a large lagoon. It was warm and sunny with a steady breeze stirring the trees and the underbrush. The sea was pale green with sparkles of light reflecting from the noonday sun like tiny diamonds. The air smelled of the ocean and tropical vegetation.

Two PT boats lay moored at a wooden pier jutting out into the bay. The majority of the pier was secured to the ocean floor. The remainder rested on rubber pontoons above the deep water. There was a natural breakwater at the mouth of the lagoon. Buoys had been set out to guide ships from running aground.

"This here is *Messalina* on your left. I named 'em after hot baby dolls. She's credited with twelve Jap barges. That's *Delilah* on your right. That little lady got herself a Jap cruiser off Bougainville. They'll do 70 knots in a calm sea. Two 20mms forward, one 40mm aft, radar, jamming gear, smoke, and two very lovely Mark 8 torpedoes. These little beauties can sink just about anything. That cargo ship should be no problem."

"Where's the rest of your men? Dutch asked."

"They're out gathering dessert for our supper tonight. All kinds uh berries and fruits grow out in the boonies, strawberries, rose apples, papaya. I love this place."

"We're set to rendezvous in three days," General Kurtz told them.

"Our bases have satellites monitoring the ships entering and leaving North Korea. *Kang Nam 8* entered the Malacca Strait this morning. We'll pinpoint her location once she crosses into the Indian Ocean."

Two days and two nights passed without incident. General Kurtz and Dutch Henry whiled away the hours walking the beaches, discussing the various problems around the world. Dozens of whales and porpoises appeared every morning. During late afternoon of the second day they observed a leopard high atop a bluff looking down at them. Sri Lanka was a paradise of colorful birds and exotic animals.

At 1300 hours on the third day, the bomb-laden vessel was 400 miles southeast.

General Kurtz gave Dutch the latest info. "She'll be due south of here around 0300. Best I can tell, she'll be about 90 miles offshore. If we leave at 2200 that'll give us plenty of time to patrol the rendezvous point. Peter has a spotter plane that'll circle the area. Once he finds the ship he'll radio her location."

"What if we can't find it in the dark?"

"I asked Peter about that. He said if we have trouble his pilot will fly above the *Kang Nam* with his lights on until we make contact."

The witching hour of ten p.m. finally arrived as a pair of patrol torpedo boats made their way out the buoyed channel and into the open sea. A panoramic silver ocean greeted them. Stars in a black void eons away glittered like tiny cosmic fireflies. The moon was full. To the east a pod of sperm whales were feeding on squid. The Indian Ocean lay silent and calm as two machines of war sought their prey.

General Kurtz was with a six-man crew on the *Messalina*. Dutch had accompanied Peter and five others on the *Delilah*. They were cruising south at 35 knots.

Realization began to dawn on Dutch Henry that placing himself in harm's way was an irresponsible act of narcissistic heroism. What if he got killed? Trudy and the kids would be left alone. General Kurtz seemed to relish these expeditions. He and Peter Engel were true warriors. But Robert had no family. He was divorced, and his mother and father were both deceased.

Their mission was indeed a serious affair.

⤸

If they failed, an enormous number of people were probably going to die in a nuclear attack. If they succeeded, they could look Saint Peter in the eye with pride on Judgment Day. From that standpoint Dutch found comfort. But these men could perform the job just as well without him. His contribution to the mission was finished once he and Kurtz finalized the Sri Lanka plan. Dutch decided then and there that his swashbuckling days were over. He was no coward, but planning and coordination were far too important for him to be risking his life on a PT boat out in the middle of the Indian Ocean. Not to mention the welfare and safety of Trudy and the three children.

⤸

Dutch whispered a silent prayer for the thirteen men, himself, and the mission.

⤸

Peter touched Dutch's arm, pointing to a group of blue whales off the port bow. Talking was difficult above the roar of the engines. A big male dove raising his flukes high in the air as he submerged beneath the waves. Dutch marveled at them, wondering how people could kill such beautiful creatures.

⤸

The world was an insane asylum, and the inmates were running the switchboard.

⤸

Two hours into their voyage they had covered 70 nautical miles. Rendezvous lay 20 miles ahead. The time was 0100 hours. They would be in position in another 40 minutes. A shooting star split the heavens above the boats. The boat captain pointed, nodding his head and grinning. Shooting stars were considered omens of good fortune.

⤳

At 0145 the PT captains pulled up alongside one another and shut down their engines. Radio silence had been maintained throughout the voyage. Peter was considering a call to the Piper Cub when his radio crackled in the chart room.

"Raven to Bluefin, can you hear me?"

"Bluefin here. I read you, Raven."

"Your party is four miles northeast of your position."

"Well done, Raven. Over and out!"

They started their motors and set a northeasterly heading at 40 knots. Five minutes later they spotted the black silhouette of a ship on the horizon. The *Kang Nam* was running with no lights. The Piper Cub flew directly over their heads, as he passed by.

"Engage jamming. Man your battle stations. Prepare to attack."

The boats separated then powered up to 50 knots. A huge column of water erupted between the two craft. Then another shell threw up a geyser close by the *Messalina*. A third round landed directly behind *Delilah*. They were at 3,000 yards and closing.

"That son of a bitch is armed to the teeth. Hang On!"

Peter spun the wheel hard left than hard right. Another shell whistled by, missing completely. At a range of 1800 yards the 20mms opened fire. Tracer rounds were pouring from the communist vessel. An explosion in front of *Delilah* drenched the crew with cold sea water.

"That bastard's got 5-inch guns!"

A shell burst directly beside the *Messalina*. Her captain veered right then left then right again, resuming his head-on assault. Twenty millimeter tracers streaked back and forth between the three combatants. Explosions, geysers of water, men yelling, and the mechanical pounding of the guns amidst the guttural roar of six 1500 HP Packard engines. A shell tore through *Delilah's* windscreen, glass cutting Peter across his chin. Dutch clung to the side of the cockpit. His life passed before his eyes. They were all scared. Dedication and adrenaline drove them on.

"Fire one!"

"Fire two!"

"Let's get the hell outta here!"

As *Delilah* began her turn they saw *Messalina* launch her torpedoes. A 5-inch shell tore through the boat's cockpit into her gas tanks. She exploded.

Seconds later the stern of the *Kang Nam* was blown completely out of the water. Another torpedo struck amidships. She blew sky high.

"Over there! Somebody's still alive."

Three men were pulled from the sea.

"Robert, can you hear me!"

The general opened his eyes. His face and hands were burned. The boat captain and a gunner were badly shaken, but all right. The others were blown to kingdom come.

"Did we get it?"

"Yes, it's gone. We scored two hits."

"That's good, that's fine. The men, are they—"

A blinding burst of energy shot out 360° beneath them deep in the sea, accompanied by a terrible rumbling. Something had detonated the atomic bomb.

Chapter Twenty-One

The Bomb

Trudy was taking a siesta on the library couch when the twins burst into the room.

"Something's wrong with daddy. He's in danger," Zelda shouted.

"What is it?"

"I don't know. All I saw was a big flash and something black."

Trudy picked up her cell phone and punched the key for a number Dutch had insisted she enter into her phone. A male voice answered.

"Is this Rico?"

"Yes, who's this?"

"This is Trudy, Dutch's wife."

"Is something wrong, Trudy?"

"Yes, I believe there is."

"What's the problem?"

"My twins are psychic. They just told me Dutch is in trouble."

"I'll make a call right away. Give me an hour and I'll get back to you."

"Thank you, Rico. I'll be waiting."

⌒

"Hit it! Get us outta here!"

Peter shoved his throttles forward. The engines thundered to life. In seconds they were running flat out from the blast area. Behind them the sea was rising. A huge black mound of water was being pushed up by the nuclear detonation hundreds of fathoms below. It exploded through the surface.

"Oh my God!"

A fireball the size of a small town began rising behind them. And with it, a wall of water rushing out in a growing circle twenty-four meters high.

"Dump everything! It's catching up!"

Dutch climbed up in a gun mount and threw a 20mm over the side. Another man did the same thing on the opposite side of the boat. They threw ammunition overboard, fire extinguishers, emergency supplies, anything they could lay their hands on. A black wall of sea water was right behind them.

Peter made a desperate decision. He spun the wheel, turning the craft around into the oncoming wave. Then he throttled down to 10 knots. A great wall of blackness loomed above them. The bow plunged into the wave. The sea swept over them. The boat rose up, up, up, until they were almost vertical. The men held on to keep from falling out. Slowly the craft settled back down as the mountain of water pushed on past.

"Sweet Jesus! You saved our lives!"

Peter was shaking so bad he couldn't speak. There was two feet of water in the crew's quarters. They had survived. Three and a half miles behind them a mushroom cloud was boiling up into the night sky. Dutch engaged the bilge pump. They sat there in silence until most of the water pumped out. They'd lost four of their comrades and the general was hurt, but they had stopped a gang of evildoers from murdering a host of innocent people. Peter went below and came up with a bottle of schnapps.

He held it overhead. "To our departed brothers."

He took a swig then passed the bottle to the general. All ten men drank. A comradery existed that hadn't been there before. Everyone began talking at once.

"The general needs medical attention. There's a first-aid kit in the head. Break out a morphine ampule and give him a shot. I'm taking us home."

⌒

Yvonne Elliman was singing "If I Can't Have You" when Dutch walked up to Peter Engle's tent and pulled back the flap. Peter was sitting in a canvas chair at a makeshift desk of ammunition crates and a sheet of plywood. A tape recorder lay on the wooden surface. Beside it sat a framed photograph of a bride in her wedding gown, a German 9mm P-38, a stack of documents, and a bottle of Schlitz. Peter was a million miles away, his eyes closed in thought.

"Hey, you okay?"

"Oh, hey yourself. Yeah, I'm cool."

"Nice song."

Peter pushed the pause button. "That's my wife's favorite song."

"Where is your wife?"

"Cecelia died four years ago. Breast cancer. She used to sing it to me. I really do miss that girl. She made all this shit worthwhile."

"I'm sorry, Peter."

"We met in Da Nang. She was an RN there during the war."

"You got any kids?"

"No, we were never blessed with children."

"I came over to tell you we're bugging out in the morning. It's been real, man."

"Dutch, you take care. I had my doubts at first, white-collar big shot an' all, but you're a good 'un."

"Coming from you, Peter, that's like receiving a Silver Star."

"Take care of the general for me. He's a good 'un too. That face of his is gonna need some work."

"Peter, I may ask for your services again someday."

"Any time, my friend. Kurtz told me what you folks do. I'm with you one hundred percent. The world is flat out going to hell in a puke bag."

"I'll never forget our boat ride."

Peter laughed. "That makes two of us. Get yourself checked for radiation when you get home."

"What about you and the fellas?"

"I got a sawbones flying in Friday. PhDs out the ass, world-famous physician. Nobody knows he's connected with us. Fine man. Collects stamps. I always send him a few wherever we go."

"If I run across any good ones, I'll send 'em your way."

"The general told me you have a wife and two kids."

"Yes, I'm very fortunate in that respect."

"Keep 'em close, Dutch. Fate has a way of fucking you when you least expect it."

Chapter Twenty-Two

Yemen

Melba Jones' hand flew to her mouth, covering her lips, when he opened the office door. The left side of his face and nose were bandaged, and he wore a black patch over his left eye. His left hand was bandaged too.

"My God, what happened to you?"

"It's a long story, Melba. Something I'm not at liberty to discuss, but it's nice seeing you again."

"Can I get you anything? Coffee, a Coke maybe?"

"I'd like some water, please. I have these pills I have to take every four hours."

Melba Jones was an attractive 44-year-old lady with raven hair, an hourglass figure, and brains. She'd been with the general eleven years. During that time she had developed a keen appreciation for the man she looked upon as a national treasure.

Melba was brilliant. She did mathematical calculations in her head, typed 95 words a minute, and possessed the ability to make people feel at home while waiting in the outer office to see General Kurtz. Kurtz wanted nothing on paper so Melba kept his itinerary in her head. Hers was a photographic memory, and she never missed a beat. She knew he went away on secret assignments, but she had no idea about Dutch Henry and the others. Melba considered herself an old maid.

The telephone rang. It was his private line. "This is Ruth. I understand you ran into some trouble."

"Four men dead and the rest of us with radiation poisoning."

"Dutch said you got burned."

"I lost some vision in my left eye. I'll have scars, but nothing serious. Besides our dead, we were lucky. Peter saved our lives. I've never been that scared in my life, Ruth."

"What happened out there?"

"The bomb was either defective or sea pressure set it off. When the blast came to the surface we were facing a wall of water 60 or 70 feet high."

"Good Lord!"

"We tried to outrun it, but we couldn't. That's when Peter turned the boat around into the wave. We nearly went over backward, but luck was with us that night."

"I don't believe you or Dutch should go on any more of these assignments. You're too valuable to the group. We all count on you."

"Dutch and I discussed that coming back. You're right. We won't be going out anymore."

"You're in your 50s, Robert. Find yourself a good woman and settle down. Younger men can handle these missions."

"Peter and his people are indispensable. They're extremely capable men."

"I'll notify Lydia we have new faces coming onboard."

"I value your judgment, Ruth. Nearly getting drowned out there changed my thinking about a lot of things. I would like to marry again. And I know just the right girl to ask."

"Good luck with that. Let me know how things turn out.

"I will, Ruth. Goodbye."

He took a deep breath to compose himself.

"Melba, would you come in here a minute, please?"

"Yes, general, what can I do for you?"

"First, I want you to stop calling me 'general' and 'sir.' My name's Robert."

"Yes, sir … I mean, Robert."

They both laughed.

"Second, will you have dinner with me tonight?"

Melba looked at General Kurtz with a gleam of affection mixed with sadness. He had never made a pass or asked her out in eleven years. She wanted to say yes, but she hesitated. She feared if she let her guard down he might hurt her, not intentionally, but because of her feelings toward him.

"I don't think I should."

"Is it because I'm older?"

"Oh no, Robert. It's nothing like that. I'm … I'm just afraid."

"Afraid of what, Melba?"

"I can't say. Please. Please, don't ask me again." She turned and went back to her desk in the outer room.

The general sat pondering what had just been said. What had he done wrong? He got up and went to ask Melba a question.

"Did I hurt your feelings?"

"No, Robert."

"Then what is it?"

Melba started to cry, her feelings leaking down her cheeks.

"Am I really that awful?"

"No, Robert. No! I care about you. I don't want to get hurt."

"I've know you what, eleven years? I couldn't get along without you. Asking you to dinner is not some scheme to get in your pants."

She wiped her tears away and smiled. "You really mean that, Robert?"

"On my honor as a Marine. I want to take you out and show you a good time, bandages and all."

"You're very sweet, General Kurtz. I accept your kind invitation."

Three weeks later Robert Kurtz proposed to Melba Jones on bended knee. Melba Jones' answer was yes.

The Welcome Center was a distinguished-looking two-story frame building situated behind a control tower that serviced a private airstrip 30 miles southwest of the port city of Zinjibar, Yemen. Tourists never went there. It was off-limits to all but a few government officials and a handful of military personnel.

It was a training center for young ladies flown there with promises of education, good jobs, and a better way of life. They came from villages around Africa and the Middle East. Others came from Germany, France, Italy, and Spain. A few were American citizens.

The region was mountainous with sparse vegetation and numerous valleys called *wadis*, which often had streams and rivers during the rainy season. Five to ten girls arrived there every third Monday.

Isabella De Luca had answered the advertisement for pretty ladies to serve as legal secretaries and couriers for diplomats and military staff. Isabella had spent her last few euros on a new dress and a pair of leather pumps. She came from a poor district on the outskirts of Rome.

When she and the others arrived, they were ushered through the front door into a reception area. Isabella was very excited. This was her way out of poverty. She was going to become somebody, a shining star in the international community of the business world.

"Put your belongings over there on that table. Take everything off but your bra and panties."

"Take off our things? What do you mean?"

The man stepped forward and stuck the girl with a riding crop. He struck her a second blow.

"Do as you're told or I'll beat the fuck outta ever one uh you cunts!"

A beauty from Thailand refused. Another man slugged her in the stomach. She fell to the tile floor clutching her midsection.

"Do it, goddamn you! Or I'll make an example of this mouthy bitch."

Isabella realized she had made a horrible mistake. They were going to be sold as sex slaves or forced into prostitution. The man with the heavy accent was Russian, Russian Mafia. Reluctantly she removed her clothing, her proud Italian breasts and round buttocks, outlined in her cotton underthings, for all the men to see.

A third man came down the line picking out the girls with the most favorable bodies. Isabella was chosen as the best one. She would fetch a handsome price. She and the others were taken to a large room upstairs. There were bunk beds and a long table with chairs in the middle of the room. The windows had steel bars over them.

⌒

"We've know about this den of inequity for some time. Why now, Lydia?" Uriah asked.

"Mimi Le Beau knows the family. Isabella and Rosie are friends."

"Russian Mafia is hardcore. We'll need some serious firepower for this."

"We have it. Peter Engle and his men are as hardcore as they come."

"Okay. Let's set it up."

⌒

The general flew back to Sri Lanka to coordinate the planning and materials needed by Peter Engle and his Black Operations personnel. The Russian Mafia was serious business. They were notorious for torture and murder. The survivors from the PT boats were almost recovered from their radiation poisoning. General Kurtz had cast off his bandages. He had minor scarring on his left cheek and nose, but nothing disfiguring. Nineteen men watched the proceedings with growing interest.

"That's about it, Peter. The airstrip is long enough for two-engine jobs. Anything bigger might run off the runway."

"We could use a Humvee. Any two-engine planes with that capability?"

"Some of the old C-47s have rear doors for offloading vehicles."

"That'll work. We got a few, but none with back doors."

"There's some out in the Arizona desert, but it'll take too long."

"Okay, the Humvee is out. We'll use one of our C-47s. The guys can go in through the mountains in a truck. They can buy one in the port city."

"I'll round up the weapons. What all do you need?"

"We have rifles and machine guns. Get me two crates uh TNT, blasting caps, and a dozen of them 30-minute timers. We lost most of our revolvers last time out. Bring me a dozen .45s with silencers. A flamethrower might come in handy if you got one. And scare up a case uh Texas Pete. Summa them field rations taste like hell."

"I'll have your stuff here in two days."

"We need to get rolling. Lydia told me they indoctrinate those girls every three weeks then out they go. We've only got two weeks left. Then they'll really be hard to find."

"She didn't tell me. How do they do that?"

"When they ain't brainwashing the girls or screwing 'em, they shoot 'em up with drugs. That way they get 'em hooked for the sex trades. Then they'll do just about anything for another fix."

"That's sick!"

"Right on! Those dirtbags need an attitude adjustment."

Three men were holding Isabella down on a bed in one of the private rooms. She fought hard, very hard, kicking and screaming, bit one on the hand, but they were too strong for her. A fourth man slid a needle into a vein in her forearm. The effect was warm and comforting. Up she soared into a psychedelic cloud. It was delightful and euphoric. She was floating in a dreamlike state. Isabella shed the sadness of being poor. The heroin made her feel secure and happy.

She felt him spread her legs apart then he entered her. She knew it was wrong, but her body betrayed her. She asked him to stop. Her mother would be mortified. But it felt good, so good. Her nipples stiffened. She couldn't help herself, lifting her hips to receive the man's lustful thrusts. Isabella was traveling down that Lost Highway.

"These bitches are all alike. Pump the dope in 'em an' they fuck like minks."

"Get your ass up. It's my turn."

Their journey through the mountains had been hazardous. Every mile or two they had to stop and clear boulders off the roadway for the truck to pass. On one sharp curve part of the road had washed out and fallen into a ravine. Getting around that took half an hour. At another juncture an aging trestle bridge appeared too rickety to support the truck. The truck got across after everyone got out and walked, except the driver. By the time they reached the entrance to the airfield they were two hours behind schedule.

A November moon glowed like a neon snowball in the pale Yemen sky. Temperatures had fallen into the 30s. The men were tense and fatigued from the stress of their journey.

"This place is fucked up! Hot in the daytime and cold at night. And it looks like we're on the damn moon. Summa them trees look like mushrooms. This place is spooky, man."

"They're called dragon's blood trees. I think they're nice."

"You'd think cow shit was nice."

"Hay burners are nice too."

"Might be guards up that driveway. How you wanna play this?"

"Everybody lies down in back. Then we drive up and ask directions like we're lost."

"Then what?"

"Shoot the motherfucker."

"Get down back there! Hang on. Here we go."

Johnny B Goode drove the vintage Ford up a rough gravel driveway toward the airfield. They'd gone 50 yards when a guard stepped out from behind a tree with an AK-47 pointed at their windshield. He wore a white parka with a white hood over his head.

"This is private property."

Johnny spoke fluent Russian. "Sir, we're lost. How do we get to Lahij?"

"Turn around and go back. Turn right. You'll see a sign down that road."

"Say, don't I know you?"

The tall Russian walked up for a closer look. He had brown eyes, bushy eyebrows, and his nose was crooked. Johnny B Goode shot him in the face.

"Drag his ass back in the trees. If he's got a cell phone, bring it."

They drove another few yards with the headlights switched off. Up ahead they could see the lights on the control tower. Each man was wearing body armor and night goggles.

"See anything?"

"No. Stay here. I'll get the tower."

They fanned out on both sides of the truck and waited. Sledgehammer found a place he liked and set up his .30 caliber machine gun. On the other side of the truck Buster Keaton did the same thing with a second .30 caliber. They watched in silence as Shane climbed up the stairs to the door on the tower. It wasn't locked. He opened it and went inside. They observed flashes from his silenced revolver. Seconds later he started back down.

"See that?"

"I got it."

The morning relief had just come out of the building behind the three story structure. Shane couldn't see the relief person because the stairwell was between him and the man. The man ambled along, taking his time smoking a cigarette.

"Got him in your sights?"

"I will in a minute."

"Remember to breathe, let it half out."

Shane froze when he saw the man coming around the bottom of the tower. The man looked up and spotted Shane. He pulled a handgun from his holster. Snafu squeezed the trigger. The silencer on the M-14 made a funny *thump*.

"Come on!"

They went running across the open field to Shane and the prone figure lying on the ground.

"Get this back in the trees. What's up top?"

"One dead Ivan. Go ahead and call Peter."

The C-47 flown by Peter Engel with five Black Ops onboard had been circling 50 miles out for the better part of an hour.

"You read me, Day Tripper?"

"Five by five, Sunny Jim."

"Come on in."

The sun was coming up in the east as they made their way toward the building. The door was locked. Johnny placed his silenced weapon against the lock and squeezed the trigger. Snafu kicked open the door. A sentry jumped up behind the reception desk. He was shot dead before he could sound the alarm.

"Stuff him in that closet back there."

The interior had been decorated by a professional designer out of

Volgograd. Pastel colors adorned the room. The floor was black-and-white tile with prints of horses and seascapes on the walls. There were comfortable couches and chairs, and tables with marble tops. A crystal chandelier hung above a beautiful cucumber wood desk. It was a believable deception for all who visited there. Hundreds of unsuspecting young women had passed through the portal of evil into a lifetime of bondage.

A door to the left of the reception desk led into a large kitchen with long wooden tables and benches. Each table had checkered tablecloths. There was an electric stove with six burners, a stainless steel refrigerator, a commercial dishwasher, a stainless steel double sink, and an Emerson freezer. Crates of onions, potatoes, and carrots were stacked against the far wall. There were cupboards and a glass china cabinet. When they opened the door, a short, baldheaded cook turned around, dropped his wooden spoon, and threw his hands in the air.

"Keep quiet and I'll let you live."

"What you want?"

"How many men upstairs?"

"They kill me if I tell."

"I'll shoot your ass if you don't. Besides, they ain't gonna be around much longer."

"You not hurt me, I tell you. I am prisoner, like ladies."

The little man wearing a white kitchen apron was shaking like a leaf. They could tell he wasn't one of the Russians. He sported a black handlebar mustache, and had the appearance of an Italian.

"How many Russians? Where are the women?"

"Ten bad men upstairs. One in tower. One in front room. One on road. One in back. Girls in big room over kitchen."

"Hillbilly, you and Shane locate that sentry out back. We got three of 'em. That leaves eleven. When Peter lands they'll be curious. We'll wait for 'em in the lobby."

The noise of the C-47 coming in to land awakened the sleeping

Russians. Johnny and the others were waiting for them in the reception area. All the lights had been turned off except for a single lamp beside the door to the right of the desk. The door opened, and three men filed out. They were wearing white parkas, combat boots, military fatigues, and carrying AK-47s. They were big, hard-looking men.

Silenced .45s spat fire again and again. The Russians pitched forward onto the black-and-white tiles. Hillbilly and Shane walked in from their backyard assignment. Shane flashed a thumbs-up to Snafu.

"Get these bastards over there behind those couches. Wait, get their parkas off. We can use them to fool the ones upstairs. And wipe up that mess."

Blacks Ops had four men positioned in the tree line with .30 caliber machine guns covering the building and the airfield. Six more were onboard the aircraft preparing to disembark. Ten Black Ops were assembled inside the two story structure on the ground floor. Seven Russians were on the second level getting dressed for breakfast.

The little cook came out from his kitchen and stood between Snafu and Johnny B Goode.

"You are good men. I not afraid anymore. You will rescue us, yes?"

"You got it, Cookie. Get back in there and cook something. They'll smell it upstairs."

"I see. Yes, I start breakfast now."

A chowhound eager for his biscuits and gravy popped through the right-hand door, surprising Johnny and the others. He yanked a pistol and fired two shots before they killed him.

"That tears it. They know we're here. You hurt bad, Snafu?"

"He nicked me in the arm. The other one hit my vest. I'm okay."

"Who is down there?"

"Relief personnel from Moscow," Johnny B Goode said in perfect Russian.

"Where's Dmitry?"

"Dmitry went outside."

"What is password?"

"I left it in the plane."

A fragmentation grenade came bouncing down the steps, followed by a second grenade. The door was blown off its hinges.

"He's at the top uh tha stairs!" Johnny yelled.

He opened fire into the overhead. The others followed his lead. They riddled the tongue-and-groove ceiling, blasting the upstairs hallway. Snafu crept up the steps. Five dead Russians lay scattered down the corridor. Snafu emptied his M-14 into the far right-hand room of the passageway.

"I kill these bitches if you don't let me go."

"It's a deal, friend. Come on out. There's a truck in the driveway. You can have it."

"You promise me?"

"I promise. I got the keys right here in my hand. You got plenty uh gas."

"No tricks, you Americans."

"No tricks, brother. Come an' get your keys."

"You give me your word?"

"Here, I'll toss 'em to ya. They's vodka in the kitchen if you want one to take with ya."

"You promise you not shoot?"

"I swear on my mother's grave."

The Russian stepped out from the women's quarters to pick up the truck keys. Snafu shot him through the heart.

"Is that what you call bein' uh Indian giver?" Johnny asked.

"No, I had my fingers crossed."

"That was righteous, man."

"I have my moments."

When they opened the door to the women's quarters they found seven girls hiding under the beds. The women were terrified from all the shooting and explosions. Each one had been drugged and raped repeatedly.

"Ladies, it's time for breakfast!" Snafu announced.

"Come on out," Shane added. "We're here to take you home."

"It's okay," Johnny assured them. "We're Americans."

One by one they crawled out from under the beds and stood before Snafu and the others. They were pretty girls. Still, they didn't know what to expect. When Hillbilly offered to assist the Thai girl, who had bruises on her legs from a beating, she pulled away.

"This isn't working," Johnny muttered. "Look, we're not going to hurt you. We'll wait downstairs in the kitchen. Get yourselves cleaned up and come on down for breakfast. Cookie's a nice fella. He'll fix whatever you want to eat."

The men left the room and waited downstairs with the cook. Ten minutes later the girls filed in and sat down at the tables. They were still frightened and nervous. Cookie went from girl to girl. For those who didn't speak English or Italian, he made signs with his hands. Pretty soon he knew what they wanted. They girls were half starved and hurting from their constant abuse. They ate everything he cooked for them and drank their milk and orange juice. Finally, a few smiles appeared.

A little black girl from Ethiopia came over to Snafu, who was sitting at his table, and stuck out her hand. He took the small, delicate fingers in his and winked at her. She leaned down and hugged his neck. The ice was broken.

Peter stood up. "You ladies get your things together. And use the bathroom. We'll be leaving here in a few minutes. We're flying back to Sri Lanka. A doctor will be there to look you over. Then we'll help you get home."

The girls chatted among themselves, some translating for the others who didn't understand. Isabella stepped forward to speak for the group. She had been raped so many times she couldn't remember.

"My friends and I wish to thank you. We all thank you from the bottom of our hearts. We've been … it's been … forgive me. I'm so ashamed."

"Honey," Peter said, "there's nothing to be ashamed about. My men understand what happened here. It wasn't your fault. I'm just thankful we got here in time."

A tear rolled down her cheek. She began to cry. The girls gathered around Isabella linking their arms around the Italian beauty. Cookie came over with a bottle of Italian brandy. He had seven small glasses on a serving tray.

"Ladies drink, please. Vecchia make you feel better."

Peter addressed the cook. "You got anything you want to take with you? It's not safe to stay here much longer."

"I have suit for church. I go get it."

"Snafu, get the flamethrower. Hillbilly, I need five packets of TNT. Set the timers for 20 minutes. Johnny, you and Pappy fuel up the plane. The rest uh you get your gear together an' get the ladies onboard."

With Cookie and the girls safely inside the aircraft, the men set about their brutish trade. Explosives were placed on the power generator, the fuel depot, the munitions bunker, and at the base of the control tower. Snafu pulled the trigger on the flamethrower through the open door of the reception area. In seconds the room was a blazing inferno.

"Time to go, people."

The C-47, with 28 passengers onboard, took most of the runway to get off the ground. Peter pulled gently on the yoke to get the aircraft above the treetops at the far end of the field. They cleared a tall pine tree, and they were airborne.

Peter circled the field once to watch the fireworks. Down below they saw the fuel dump go up in a huge ball of fire. Then the control tower splintered and crashed to the ground. Other explosives began going off. Flames were leaping high in the air above the burning building.

The flight to Sri Lanka would last the remainder of the day. The girls settled down, and some slept peacefully for the first time in two weeks. Isabella was sitting beside Snafu. She reached over and took his hand in hers. He looked over at the beautiful Italian. She smiled back at him, placing her head on his shoulder.

"What's your name, sugarplum?"

"Isabella De Luca. I'm from Italy. What is your name?"

"Clem Kadiddlehopper."

She giggled, looking at him with amusement. "It is not."

"My name is Jim, Jimmy Angel. My friends call me Snafu."

"That's a funny name. What does it mean?"

"Situation normal, all fucked up."

"You don't ... well … seem that way to me."

"It's just a nickname. Most of the guys have nicknames."

"I like Jimmy better."

"You're a very pretty lady, Isabella."

"Thank you, Jimmy. I can tell you're a gentleman. You're not all hands like those boys back home. I like talking with you."

"My mama and daddy raised me up proper. I'm from Tennessee."

"What's it like in Tennessee?"

"I'm from a place called Louisville. There's a big river there. That's the Tennessee River. It's very green with lots of trees, and the people are as friendly as all get out."

"Maybe you'll come visit me sometime? I live with my mother in Prati. That's not far from Rome. I could show you around. Mama would love cooking for you."

"I have two weeks off for Christmas."

"Yes, that would be lovely."

"*You're* lovely, Isabella."

"You don't think less of me because of … back there?"

"No, sugar. You're just perfect the way you are."

"I like you very much, Jimmy Angel."

Snafu leaned over and gave her a peck on the cheek. Isabella placed her arms around his neck and kissed him. He spread their blanket over her to keep her warm. She snuggled down, placing her head in his lap. She was soon fast asleep. Snafu leaned back, closing his eyes, smiling, and thanking God for the beautiful young lady who had just come into his life.

Chapter Twenty-Three

Sherlock Holmes

June 2010

"Ruth Townsend called this morning. They're at it again, Boo."

"At what, Lydia?"

"That Kim Jong fatso has two bombs going out. They're bound for Iran, same as last time. Fatso is as mad as a bag of ferrets."

"Does the general know?"

"Not yet. Neither does Dutch Henry."

"You better get on the phone. Two bombs could wipe out Israel. We need Peter Engel again."

⌒

"We barely got out with our lives last time, Dutch. This sounds even worse." Peter was concerned for his men.

"It is worse. They have a destroyer escorting that cargo ship."

"Where did those clowns get a destroyer?"

"It's an old Russian Kashin class. Not much by modern standards, but it does have an array of weapons platforms. She can do 33 knots and has a range of 4,000 miles. The distance from North Korea to Iran is 7,500, give or take, so the North Koreans will have a mothership out there in the South China Sea or the Indian Ocean or maybe both."

"How the hell are we gonna deal with a destroyer?"

"I don't know. Let's hope the general comes up with something."

⁓

"I've found a solution for my, you know … my problem," Zephyr announced.

Zelda arched an eyebrow. "And what might that be, Miss Horny Britches?"

"Mathew Ferguson."

"My stars and garters!"

"It's not like that, Zel. He cares for me. And I feel the same way about him."

"When did this come about?"

"I've been seeing him off and on for a month now. I wasn't sure at first so I didn't want you or Mom and Daddy to know. I really do like him, Zelda. I think I'm in love."

"I've been having orgasms all over the place. And I thought you were just abusing your Ladies Home Companion."

Zephyr laughed. "It's amazing the way you and I experience one another's climaxes. I think it's wonderful."

"I do too, but what does Mathew say about all this?"

"He wants me to marry him."

"Wow! I like Mathew, but a month isn't long enough. You need to wait and make sure."

"I told him that. I told him we have to wait a year."

"I hope it lasts forever, big sister.

"You know something? I never realized how nice sex could be. It's really like magic."

"Maybe I'll find a nice man someday. What I remember from our kidnapping was just awful."

"You will, Zelda. A wonderful man will come along. I know he will."

"Keep me posted. I'll say a prayer for you guys."

"Thank you. We'll keep our eyes open for a nice fella for you, little sister."

"That would be super."

General Kurtz tapped a finger on his desktop. "I think it's time we brought the Israelis in on this. Their survival is on the line, Peter."

"I agree. And they have those anti-ship missiles."

"I researched them. They're called Gabriel IV. They've been upgraded four times. They have a 530-pound warhead and a range of 120 miles. Fire and forget. Gabriel translates 'man of God' or 'strength of God.' Gabriel was the angel who told Mary she would give birth to Jesus."

"That Gabriel sounds like one tough customer. How will we keep from hitting the other ship?"

"Good question. They're heat-seeking. I guess we'll have to get in close and launch directly at the target. Otherwise it might lock on the wrong one."

"Right! We want that ship intact, general."

"I'll get with Uriah on this. We have to convince the Israelis about those bombs."

"Hell, they already have enough nuclear stuff to blow away the Middle East. It shouldn't take that much convincing."

You're probably right, but their leaders are very cautious."

"I would be too if I were in their shoes. They can't afford mistakes. It could cost them their country. When are you leaving for London?"

"Early tomorrow morning. Lydia and Uriah are expecting me."

"Ask Uriah to round up some extra help. Capturing that ship is gonna take some doing."

⸺

"It would be aces if we could go straight to the top and skip the naffers, general."

"Lydia is right. Do you have a connection that could get you in to see Netanyahu?"

"Bobbi … he's friends with Bibi. I'll call him." Uriah said.

"You can explain everything about North Korea to the Prime Minister – how the CIA gets their information, and why we want those bombs. But be careful about our personal roles in this. Netanyahu doesn't need to be burdened with it. Nor does he need to know."

"I'm going with you, Boo. Bobbi likes me. I'll put on me war paint and show off me knockers."

"She's utterly devious, general. And I love the wench."

"And a brilliant lady you are, Lydia. Those Israeli officers will be impressed with you. But be careful out there. You're both indispensable to the group."

⸺

The meeting with Bobbi went perfectly. He saw immediately the dire threat of the situation. It took Bobbi one hour to contact the Prime Minister. Bobbi assured the PM that Lydia and Uriah were genuine. He explained briefly about the North Korean ships, and the nuclear threat to Israel.

Lydia and Uriah flew to Tel Aviv the following morning. They were met at the Ben Gurion Airport and escorted to the headquarters of General Jebediah Abram. The man was of average height and build, with tufts of white hair on the sides of his balding head. He was fifty-eight and weighed no more than 150 pounds. His face was lined and craggy from years of responsibility and making life-and-death decisions. He'd lost his left arm in the Yom Kippur War.

The general turned out to be an intellectual. He saw to the heart of matters right off the bat. He spoke briefly about the many threats facing Israel, and America's role as leader of the free world.

When told about the bombs he became focused, asking to know everything about the two ships. Uriah told him about the first interception in the Indian Ocean which resulted in a nuclear detonation with four men killed. The general acknowledged they were aware an explosion had taken place, but they were unable to determine who was responsible or where it came from.

A second shipment was to take place within the month. Uriah elaborated about the enemy ships, and the spy they had inside the North Korean compound. He explained that his comrades planned to capture the cargo ship and steal the atomic bombs. When asked why Uriah's friends wanted the bombs, Uriah answered truthfully. They could be deployed at a later date against the enemies of Israel and the West. He explained there would be no political roadblocks if that decision ever came to pass.

Discussions carried over into the evening hours. An air force colonel was called in for his professional opinion. Two members of the Knesset who supported Netanyahu and his stance on Palestine were summoned. All agreed that the Kim Jong ships must be stopped at all costs. Then Lydia asked about the Gabriel IV.

Colonel Gavri suggested using the F-21 Kfir fighter. It had a range of 800 miles and an integrated electronics system that could defeat any missile the North Korean destroyer might throw at them. A tanker plane would be dispatched for refueling the fighters.

The men understood the need for secrecy regarding Uriah and Lydia and the pending attack on the North Korean warship. The stage was set. A sea battle was about to take place which could alter the fate of Israel and the entire Western World.

⤳

"What worries me are those 76mm guns. I've been reading while you were gone. They got two twin mounts, fore and aft. Range is eleven miles, 45 rounds per minute. Those flyboys better be careful. They can defeat the SAM missiles, but plain ole artillery coming your way is something else. We better be careful our damn selves!"

"I won't be going with you, Peter."

"You got no business out there, general. The group needs you in Washington to keep the ball rolling. The boys and I will handle this shit. By the way, thank you for what you did for those fellows that got killed. Their families really appreciate the money."

"We have a source in London. Anybody that gets hurt will receive proper medical attention. Anyone killed, their family will be provided for."

"If I don't like somebody, I steer clear of 'em. How do you tolerate those numbskulls in Smoke and Mirrors Land? I couldn't do it."

"It comes with the job, Peter. Sometimes you just ignore their mistakes. Other times you have to follow through, like those Rules of Engagement from the Obama White House."

"I understand a lot of our boys got killed because of that."

"That's true. We should have pulled out of Iraq years ago. After we whipped Saddam we could have handed the place back to the Iraqi Army and come home. But Donald Rumsfeld and Ambassador Bremer were a pair of know-it-alls. They ordered the Iraqi Army disbanded. That resulted in 300,000 Iraqi soldiers, with explosives and automatic weapons, out of a job.

"General Franks advised the DOD to keep the army and use them to help stabilize the country. They spoke the language and knew the people. But Bremer and Rumsfeld disbanded the army in spite of Tommy's advice. That was pure stupidity. General Franks said to hell with it and quit. Then Iraq went down the tubes. Bush offered Franks the flag position at the Pentagon. Tommy told him 'No Thanks,' and retired. Then Bush got us into Afghanistan. Obama keeps the pot boiling all over the Middle East. It's Vietnam over and over again."

"Obama strikes me as a lost ball in high weeds."

"A lot of people think that. I believe he's a very cunning individual. Intelligence can't decide if the president is a Muslim or what he is. All his records have been sealed or destroyed. George Soros took care of that. We know about his ties with CAIR in Washington and the Muslim Brotherhood in Egypt. But one thing everyone agrees on, Barack Obama is one hundred percent anti-USA."

"How do you know that?"

General Kurtz pulled out a file from his leather briefcase. "These are notes I took at an Intelligence briefing at Camp LeJeune last year on Barack Obama's early history. Melba corrected my spelling and typed them for me.

"His record goes on and on, but here's the bottom line. Barack was influenced all his young life by Muslims and left wingers. Ann Dunham met Barack Obama, Sr. at the University of Hawaii in 1960. She got pregnant so they married in 1961. Ann divorced him in 1964. Frank Davis, Barack's adolescent counselor, was a card-carrying communist. Stanley Dunham, Ann's father, was a socialist. He served honorably in World War Two. Lolo Soetoro, Barrack's stepfather, was a Muslim. Lolo was an easygoing fella. Barack's mother, Ann, was an atheist and a cultural Marxist. Jeremiah Wright, Obama's pastor, was a Black Nationalist and a former Muslim."

"Snafu studies politics and world history. He tells me stuff I wish I didn't know. How the hell did this man get elected, general?"

"My father used to tell me about the communist movement in America back in the '30s. They've been trying to take control of our education system ever since Franklin Roosevelt was in office. Hitler said, 'He who controls the youth, controls the future.' The Democrats, the welfare crowd, and the usual menagerie of progressive misfits elected Obama."

"Sounds like Uncle Sam got buggered, good and proper!"

"Yes, and they've brainwashed half the country with their redistribution of the wealth bullshit. Barack trained in Chicago as a community organizer. Back in the 1930s Saul Alinsky invented community organizing, calling on black churches and poor black neighborhoods. Alinsky was a communist just like our old friend, George Soros. He wrote a book called *Rules for Radicals*. Saul Alinsky died in 1972."

"That Soros bastard should be jailed or deported."

"That, he should."

The general flipped through a few more pages. "These are some of Barack's supporters who helped him along the way to the White House.

"Gregory Galluzzo was a Jesuit priest who pushed Saul Alinsky's left-wing agenda on the Catholic Church. He and Obama were heavily involved with the Alinsky inspired Gamaliel Foundation in Chicago. That effort eventually failed.

"George McNight was a Northwestern University professor. He was a mentor to Barack during his community organizing days. McNight recommended Obama to Harvard Law School.

"Ken Rolling was the administrator for the Midwest Academy. He helped fund Obama's work as a community organizer. Rolling worked with Obama on the Woods Fund, and ran the Chicago Annenberg Challenge managed by Obama and Bill Ayres. Millions went into community organizing through the Annenberg project.

"Bill Ayres was a close associate of Obama. They lived in Hyde Park. He was the former leader of the Weather Underground. *Dreams from My Father* was a fairy tale of half-truths and fiction written by Ayres, and passed off as being written by Obama.

"Alice Palmer was a Soviet sympathizer who stepped down from her Illinois Senate seat to run for Congress. She endorsed Barack for her senate seat. The organizers got behind Obama and he won.

"Jeremiah Wright served as his pastor for twenty years. He was Obama's surrogate father in Chicago until he ran for president in 2007. Jeremiah married Michelle and Barack.

ACORN is the Association of Community Organizations for Reform Now. Barack trained some of their staff. ACORN was Saul Alinsky on steroids. Congress shut down their funding in 2009."

"This is not good, general. Does it get any better?"

"No, the shit just gets deeper. Congress is as screwed up as Hogan's goat. A number of them don't have the brains God gave a goose. They seldom read a bill before voting on it. Others are there for the power and the recognition. Not to mention all those cocktail parties. Many of them are socialists. The Pentagon is full up with bonehead appointees. Some couldn't make a right decision if Russian tanks were rolling down Pennsylvania Avenue."

"Like I said, I couldn't handle your job."

"Let's concentrate on those nukes. How are we going to get on that boat?"

"I been workin' on that. If the flyboys strafe the decks a few times, that'll clear out the topside gunners. But I ain't figured out yet how to get onboard."

"I like your strafing notion. With those guns knocked out we might use our PT boats or maybe something bigger. You got anything like that?"

"We got a Chinese gunboat we took off some opium smugglers two years ago. Our mechanics souped it up some. It'll do 38 or 39 knots."

"How big is it?"

"It's about 120 feet long. We could mount some 40 mms on that sucker. A Gatling gun would be the icing on the cake."

"Mister Engel, I think you just solved our problem."

Karl Rove, chief Republican consul and his RNC confederates, Washington's RINO country-club elite, lost control of Congress in 2006. Then they lost the White House in 2008. That was accomplished by serving up political pablum to Reaganite conservatives. The "Maverick," John McCain, was in truth a Republican in name only himself. The only thing good about McCain's political campaign was Sarah Palin, who was told to smile, be friendly, and say what they told her to say.

Barack Hussein Obama was never vetted, nor was he held accountable for his questionable relationships with people of dubious character and backgrounds. He was heartily endorsed by George Soros, the DNC, and the major news networks. Obama rolled over Senator McCain to an easy victory. Hope and Change had come to America.

Democrats argued that the president's $819 billion 2009 Stimulus Package was a great success. Republicans said just the opposite. That much of it went to the president's union supporters which kept them afloat while the rest of the country was mired in recession. Whatever the case, the recession continued on while millions lost their jobs, their homes, their automobiles, and their health insurance.

The British Petroleum Deepwater Horizon disaster in the Gulf of Mexico in 2010 gave insight into President Obama's managerial skills. For weeks he dithered, claiming it was BP's job to fix the problem. Meanwhile millions of gallons of toxic oil gushed from the ocean floor, killing fish and wildlife, and wrecking the Gulf's tourist trade. Eighty-seven days later the blowout was finally capped.

A president had been established. Barack Obama was not a man of decisive action. Decision-making was not his forte. Executing the president's health care mandate, Nancy Pelosi, Harry Reid, and the DC Democrats rammed Obama Care down the throats of the American people. In doing so, Nancy Pelosi exclaimed, "We have to pass the bill so that you can find out what is in it."

Karl Rove and Company stepped in it again in 2012. Mitt Romney was another Republican in name only the RNC presented to the American electorate as their presidential nominee. Romney never challenged Barack Obama's socialist agenda. Nor did he sell himself as a man of the people. And he never pursued the Obama-Clinton Benghazi cover-up. Uncle Sam and Lady Liberty were in for a rough and bumpy ride.

❧

It was 1730 hours. Outside the temperature was 82 degrees. Sea swells were breaking off in whitecaps. The ocean was growing rough and choppy. A bright sun hung low in the west. There was a cool breeze blowing from the SE. Storm clouds appeared to the north, low above a dark horizon.

Snafu sat at the helm awaiting a radio call from the Israeli pilots flying the F-21s. Their rendezvous with the North Korean destroyer was due in 18 minutes. Snafu and the crew were 20 miles north of the rendezvous point, drifting on a windswept sea.

Peter had fallen ill from his Agent Orange poisoning. He was seated in an easy chair beside Snafu behind the pilot house windows. Johnny B Goode stood on the other side of Snafu with a pair of binoculars draped around his neck.

Out front, on the port side of the ship, Shane and three other men manned a 40 mm Bofors gun. Sledgehammer and three more Black Ops waited on the starboard side with their 40 mm. Buster Keaton, Hillbilly, and Pappy were on the 20 mm Gatling gun between the two anti-aircraft weapons. The rest waited on deck with grappling hooks or were down below in the engine room. Breaking waves hurled ocean spray across the rolling deck of the gunboat.

Peter was dozing, dreaming of his days in Vietnam where he met his wife, Cecelia. He and a buddy had gone to see the Bob Hope Christmas Special. He was ogling Raquel Welch when the lady sitting next to him punched him in the ribs.

"You naughty boy," she said, laughing merrily.

When Peter turned to address the person bugging him, his heart jumped up into his throat. A gorgeous RN sat there, smiling. Auburn hair, brown eyes, and the prettiest face ever to steal a man's heart away. It was love at first sight, both for Peter and Cecelia.

He dreamed about his close calls in the jungle, and that time another Marine stepped on a land mine and he caught some of the shrapnel. Peter had insisted that he be sent to the hospital where Cecelia nursed. He adamantly refused to be treated anywhere else. After he was up and around, the hospital chaplain married them in the hospital chapel.

They honeymooned for five glorious days: picnics and swimming on China Beach, sightseeing the Marble Mountains, dinner and dancing in downtown Da Nang. It was a new beginning for two young lovers in a war-torn land a long ways from Disneyland. Then it was back to work for the newlyweds. Peter would always remember Cecelia singing to him, "If I Can't Have You."

"Peter! Wake up! I hear the planes."

Peter opened his eyes. To the east they could hear the sound of the fighter bombers on their way to the North Korean destroyer.

"Sky King to Day Tripper … Do you copy?"

"Five by five, Sky King. We're on the way."

Snafu engaged the engine, pushing the throttle forward to 35 knots. In the distance they heard two muffled explosions, followed by an extremely loud "*BOOM!*" Caught off guard, the destroyer had blown up when a third Gabriel IV struck her aft magazine.

They could see tracers flying back and forth in the sky. Gunfire from the cargo ship raged for several minutes then stopped. The Israeli pilots flew over the gunboat, waggling their wings, on their way home. Snafu approached the damaged freighter with caution. Two machine guns opened fire from upper windows in the ship's tower, shooting out the glass on the bridge of the Chinese gunboat.

The Gatling gun crew engaged. Thirty-three 20mm rounds per second blew out the window frames, the ship's plating, and everything around the tower windows. Both machine guns fell silent. Snafu pulled up alongside, and the deck gang hurled their grappling hooks. In seconds they were onboard the North Korean vessel. Stonewall raced up to the bridge and shut down the engine.

Dead men lay everywhere. The bridge tower and the main deck, fore and aft, were shot full of holes. Six long-range 5-inch batteries were mounted on the ship, three on each side. Loose shells rolled lazily about the heaving deck. There were eight anti-aircraft guns as well, four on either side. Numerous machine guns lay hither and yon and up on the bridge platforms.

They found the bombs underneath the stairwell inside the main hatch. Their white ceramic casings glistened eerily in the fading afternoon light.

"Will ya look at that?"

"Creepy, ain't they?"

"Yes, sir. And to think those crazy Iranians might uh got um."

Johnny B Goode appeared. "Guys, we got a problem."

Sledgehammer swung around. "What's wrong?'

"Some uh them shells went straight through. The ship is sinking."

"Get busy on that crane yonder, boys," Snafu yelled. "We'll load 'em on the gunboat."

"Roll 'em out, dudes. This ain't no time for lollygaggin'," Johnny told the crew.

The atomic bombs weighed 2,372 pounds apiece. It didn't take long to hoist them over onto the deck of the gunboat, less than twenty minutes. They were lashed down securely and covered over with tarpaulins. By then the front of the cargo ship was down at the bow four and a half feet. Her steel beams were groaning and popping. As they were abandoning the ship an old man and a boy ran out on the deck. They'd been in hiding in a paint locker.

"No shoot, please. No Shoot."

"Come on, old timer. This tub's goin' down."

The old man and the boy made a running jump from the sinking ship onto the deck of the Chinese craft. Shane and four others were busy hacking away with axes and machetes to cut the grappling lines.

"Buster, put a few rounds in the ass end. Let the air out."

Pom! Pom! Pom! Pom!

Minutes later the stern of the ship rose high in the air. Then she began a steady slide down into the sea. And she was gone. A rush of bubbles came up. Bodies and debris rose to the surface. Soon all that was left was wreckage, floating dead men, and the rolling ocean.

"You speak English, Gran-paw?"

"Some, a little."

"What were you doing on that boat?"

"Me and boy cook and wash dishes. They keep us prisoners."

"You want to come to America?"

"Yes, please. Boy is grandson. Family all dead."

"You hungry?"

"Yes, please. Boy hungry."

"Hillbilly, take 'em inside. Give 'em a sandwich an' a Coke."

"Come on, son. What's your name?"

"Boy's name Chin-Sun."

⸎

When Snafu returned to the pilot house, he stopped dead in his tracks, staring at Peter. There was a large pool of blood beneath Peter's chair. He had blood down the front of his pea jacket, and all over his hands.

"Peter! What happened?"

Peter Engle opened his eyes. "Piece uh glass cut me."

"You need a transfusion. I'll get Buster. He knows what to do."

"No, Jimmy. Leave me be. I was dying anyway."

"But, sir, the men need you to lead them."

"No, Jimmy. You're the boss now. Johnny will serve you like he helped me."

"Peter, I can't do this."

"Snafu, listen to me! I been dying a piece at a time ever since Vietnam. Agent Orange is bad stuff. Those ass wipes at the Pentagon didn't want to admit it made us sick. Fuck them! I've had a lot uh misery here lately. I want it this way, Jimmy."

Snafu went to the door and called the men. All eighteen crowded into the pilot house.

"Boys, I'm gonna leave ya in a little while. A piece uh glass got me. Agent Orange is eating my lunch so this is the way I want to check out. Doc tells me I'll be dead in a few months anyway. It's been my privilege and my good fortune to have served with you men. Each one of you is a tribute to your country and that uniform you wear. You are the best of the best.

"Listen up now. Snafu is your new boss. Johnny, you help Jimmy the way you helped me."

"Yes, Peter. I'll watch over Angel and the fellas for ya."

"General Kurtz and Dutch Henry will be calling on you from time to time. Work with 'em. They represent everything good about America."

Several of the men had tears running down their cheeks.

Hillbilly knelt down beside Peter's blood-soaked chair. He took Peter's bloody hand in his. "I'm sure gonna miss you, sir. You been like a daddy to me. You been like a daddy to ever' man here."

"You're a good lad, son. Keep your nose clean. Don't take no wooden nickels."

Sledgehammer began to weep openly.

"I'm mighty tired now. Come shake my hand then get back to work. You got them bombs to look after. I'm headin' up for Glory to see my pretty wife, Miss Cecelia."

One by one they filed by, shaking Peter's feeble hand, saying their final goodbyes. Soon everyone had left the cabin except Snafu and Johnny B Goode. A short while later Peter Engle took leave of his Black Operations brothers. Up ahead he could see a bright and shining light. Captain Engle passed away with a contented smile on his face.

⌒

General Kurtz, Dutch Henry, and Ruth Townsend were seated around a table in Ruth's office at Langley, Virginia. Ruth had ordered coffee and cherry pie brought up from the cafeteria. The table sat in front of a large window overlooking the Potomac River. Leaves had turned their bright autumn colors. It was early November, a clear and sunny morning. A mockingbird was fluttering about a sugar maple down beneath the window ledge.

"Peter and the gang sure pulled this one off," Dutch said. "I'm gonna miss that man. He was … I don't know, he was just different. I never met anybody quite like him before."

"He was a loyal American, right down to his cowboy boots," General Kurtz declared. "In ways he reminded me of Winston Peters."

Ruth sighed. "I wish I'd known Peter Engel. That funeral sure was something, all those men pounding their badges into his casket."

"The one they call Snafu told me Peter got cut by a piece of glass. Agent Orange was killing him. Snafu said he'd gotten a lot worse lately. Peter just sat there in his chair and bled to death. He wanted to be with his wife. Cecelia passed away five years ago."

"Don't tell me anymore," Ruth murmured. "You'll make me cry."

"I'm sorry. Let's get down to business."

"Where can we store those things, general? They're too valuable to leave in a warehouse or some military base."

Ruth looked at Dutch. "You mentioned you might have a place."

"My basement, if you guys agree. It's unfinished and dry as a chip.

I keep my mower and garden tools down there. There's a double door, plenty wide enough to get the bombs inside. I'll need a small AC unit to keep the bombs cool, a dehumidifier to control the humidity, and some extra insulation."

"What about your family?"

"I asked Trudy about storing those things. She told me she's proud to be a part of our organization. We'll dream up something to tell the twins."

General Kurtz voiced a concern. "Uranium bombs attract moisture from the atmosphere. We don't want rust getting inside those casings. You'll need a gas generator in case the electricity goes out."

"Build a secure room for the bombs. Insulate everything," Ruth suggested.

"Sounds like a plan."

"When the bombs get here, our people can manage the truck and the lifting equipment. They can build that bomb room while they're in town, Dutch."

"Snafu said they'd be here Thursday. They're bringing them over on two cargo planes. I've made arrangements for the offload at Dobbins Air Base in Marietta. A friend of mine is taking care of things. Colonel Carroll is one of us."

Ruth smiled. "This is some hoot. You'll be sitting on 80,000 tons of nuclear throw weight. Those bombs are 40,000 apiece. That's twice Fat Man's power at Nagasaki."

"I flew a technician over to make sure they're safe, Dutch. Rodney told me they have long lifespans. Just the same, they should be inspected every few months."

"I've been thinking," Dutch began. "Capitol Hill has taken on the role of the Evil Empire ever since the Soviet Union went under. Much of Congress is for sale to the highest bidder. Obama is our Manchurian Candidate, anti-USA right down to his Rules for Radicals hymnal. Every department head he appointed is some kind of tax-and-spend socialist. The DOJ has judges legislating out of thin air. Then there's our Department of Education promoting Lenin and Marx in our children's classrooms."

"I don't like the sound of this." Ruth touched his arm.

The general looked down at his empty plate. "I hope it never comes to that. A lot of innocent people would die. If we could marshal some kind of evacuation plan, that would save thousands of lives. And the tourists, Dutch, the tourists are always there."

Dutch held up his hand. "Hold on, I'm not talking about blowing away the capital. What are your thoughts about a military takeover on a temporary footing?"

"I've thought about it. We all have. No question Obama is a quisling. His czars are like you said. So are those congressmen. I say ride it out until 2016."

"I'll second that, general," Ruth added. "If Hillary or some other socialist gets elected, I say go for it. If a Republican gets in and it's the same old RINO crap, send the troops in and clean house."

Dutch agreed. "The year 2016 sounds fine to me."

"First thing we should concentrate on is finding suitable people to manage the country, get it back on a business footing. Reagan was good at that. Allen West is a good man. I know Allen. So are Scott Baker and Rick Perry. Thomas Sowell and Bobby Jindal are good too. Trey Gowdy would make a fine attorney general. Donald Trump is a business wizard. There are lots of good men and women out there who can turn this country around."

"I like your suggestions, general. I think we should bring back the draft too. Get those young boys off the streets and teach them something. Then settle welfare. The states can create jobs for those welfare recipients. Most of them are able-bodied. They can work. Get the Feds out of the picture. The states can manage their own affairs. That's the way our forefathers intended it."

"Amen, Ruth. Our citizens are sick and tired of Congress and

Barack Obama. And the country doesn't need another Bush or Clinton. Boehner and McConnell have to go too. Those two are Judas goats. We need term limits. With the right changes, this economy could make the rest of the world look like it's standing still."

"If a takeover appears to be our best strategy, give me 90 days. I'll put a division in place. Rank-and-file soldiers view the White House and Congress as the real enemy, more so than the Taliban or al Qaeda. Corporate America could work wonders with the unions, the lawyers, and the EPA off their backs. They could bring back our industrial base from overseas."

"Part of my intelligence community despises Washington," Ruth admitted. "They don't trust Obama or what they say on Capitol Hill. I could push some buttons, make a few calls. When the time comes, my people will be ready."

"What if our plans fail? Would you recommend using the bomb then, Ruth?"

"That's a terrible responsibility. What do you think, Robert?"

"I'd have to say yes, if it looks like we're losing the country. We couldn't stand by and do nothing. But we'll have to figure a way to get some of the people out."

"What about China and Russia?" Dutch asked.

"Our Armed Forces would have to be in DEFCON mode. There are specialists I'll need at the Pentagon. I can get them out of Washington beforehand. The Russians and the Chinese will stand down if they know we mean business."

"A lot of people want us to fail. We're last man standing against the socialist agenda for One World Government. The Middle East is going to hell in a handbasket. That's part of the plan," Ruth explained. "Once they control Middle Eastern oil, they'll have half the world under their thumb."

"The president is redistributing the nation's wealth with that Cloward-Piven garbage. We can survive that ass until he leaves office.

Then if nothing changes, I say give it to the group." Dutch was visibly disgusted over Washington's self-serving menagerie of hypocrites.

"I agree. Congress is unfit to govern. Some of them are as bad as Obama. The fate of our republic should rest with the people who love America."

General Kurtz gazed sadly at his friends.

"Sir Author Conan Doyle is one of my favorite authors. I used to read his stories at night to help me fall asleep. Doyle patterned Sherlock Holmes after Doctor Joseph Bell of the Royal Infirmary of Edinburgh in Scotland. Doctor Bell was an amazing physician. He could observe a patient and tell what was ailing him, and what he did for a living.

"The Marine Corps Combat Development Command teaches this approach in top-down logic. Sun Tzu was like that. So was Hermann Balck, a brilliant panzer commander on the Eastern Front.

"All I see in Washington is wickedness and corruption.

"Obama's White House is in cahoots with the Muslim Brotherhood, Cuba, Iran, and you name it. The media is run by six giant corporations that promote socialism against capitalism. Green Energy operates on the same offensive principal. Congress, Democrats and Republicans, are a two-faced herd of socialist windbags. They aren't loyal to anyone but themselves and whoever gives them money. Joe McCarthy used to wave a piece of paper in the air saying he had the names of communists in the US Government. Today that list would be a yard long, hell, maybe six feet.

"Worst of all are those lobbyists and bureaucrats. They're embedded in Capitol Hill like maggots in a battlefield corpse. Socialism and communism, there isn't a dime's worth of difference between the two. Little Boy and Fat Man cost 250,000 lives. That saved a million Allied troops and five to ten million Japanese.

"A bomb at ground level would cause less collateral damage."

London, England

"Boo, they did it! We have two atomic bombs at our disposal."

"My God, Lydia. That's frightening."

"Yes, Boo, and the power that comes with it."

"I guess … oh my … I guess I understand now how my people feel about their nuclear arsenal."

"Yes, love, it's a ghastly responsibility. But without it Israel would be destroyed. The same is true for England and the United States. It's true for all the Western Powers."

"You're a visionary, Lydia. Sometimes you remind me of Golda."

"Boo, if Washington is taken over by those progressive bastards and a military coup fails, Ruth told me she and General Kurtz will ask the group for a vote. If the situation is voted tits up, so long Fifth Column, USA."

Contact the Author

To Contact the Author, visit his website at:
McAnallyFlatsPress.com

Or write to him via the publisher at:

Larry Henry
c/o McAnally Flats Press
4809 Riversedge Road
Louisville, TN 37777